GHOST PLANE OF BLACKWATER

Ghost Plane
of
Blackwater

William F. Hallstead

A VOYAGER BOOK

HARCOURT BRACE JOVANOVICH

NEW YORK AND LONDON

Library of Congress Cataloging in Publication Data

Hallstead, William F
Ghost plane of Blackwater.

(A Voyager book, AVB 95)
SUMMARY: Two pilots search for a bomber lost over
a South Carolina swamp.
[1. Air pilots—Fiction.   2. Mystery and detective
stories]   I. Title.
[PZ7.H1655Gh]   [Fic]   74-17071
ISBN 0-15-634730-X

First Voyager edition 1975
A B C D E F G H I J

GHOST PLANE OF BLACKWATER

1

THE PLACE WAS JUST PLAIN SPOOKY, BUT I was ashamed to admit it to myself.

At nineteen, you're supposed to be above such thoughts, but I couldn't shake the feeling that the dark swamps edging Interstate 95 hid a lot of things that I'd just as soon not tangle with, to be truthful about it. Dead tree trunks jutted from tar-colored water to gleam silver against the matted dark underbrush. An egret glided along the highway, bending its long white neck toward me as I drummed past at sixty miles an hour.

What else lived in these swamps? Alligators, I'd read, even though they were getting pretty scarce. Turtles, little dark brown marsh rabbits, plenty of cottonmouth moccasins—those tough, chunky water snakes with a bite that could knock you down, maybe for good.

This was an eerie part of South Carolina, and the late afternoon storm building off in the west didn't help a bit. Its leading edge had blotted out the setting sun half an hour ago. Now the storm's long black arms reached over the highway and gave what was left of the day a greenish tint.

No, I didn't like this place, and I was glad I was just driving through it, not stopping.

Then, right in the middle of this gnarled and twisted wasteland, I saw the sign.

"Oh, no! Not here!" But here it was, all right. EXIT FOR BLACKWATER.

A little shiver went skipping along my back. "Come on, Greg Stewart," I said out loud. "You wanted an agricultural flying job. It happens to be here, and that's that."

I was tempted to glance into the back seat of my old sedan to make sure nobody had heard me talking to myself, but I knew nobody was there. I'd driven five hundred miles from Pennsylvania strictly alone; the farthest I'd ever been from home, come to think of it. My folks didn't think so much of the idea, but when you're six feet tall, old enough to vote, and a full-fledged commercial pilot, you don't feel too much like turning down a job offer just because your dad thinks South Carolina is a long way off.

Of course, I wasn't exactly as confident as I'd let him think, but I wasn't going to back down. Not after I'd slaved in the grease pits of Cartwright's garage for three summers to scratch up flying-lesson money. Not after I'd worked every day after school and on weekends in Dad's hardware store to pay for all the hours it takes to get a commercial ticket.

Now that I found myself deep in the swampy south where

I didn't know a soul, with a stormy night closing in fast, I wasn't so sure I really knew what I was doing after all.

The side road was a narrow strip of blacktop that curved away from the interstate highway to wind through the swampland. Lightning flared a few miles ahead. I was driving west, right into it. Then daylight began to give up altogether, and I clicked up the highbeams. I followed the blacktop road deeper and deeper into tangled wilderness. When a long jagged wire of lightning flared into the ground just beyond the trees to my right, I had to hit the brakes until I could see again.

The wind came in a rush. It scattered handfuls of bright green leaves through the headlight beams. Then its full force rolled out of the blackest corner of the swamps like a low-flying bomber, all engines at full throttle. It smacked the car like a fist. I wrenched the wheel to the left, and the wheels bounced out of the soft gravel and found the pavement again. The first big drops clanked on the hood.

I almost missed the fork in the road, and I could barely see the directional sign. I rolled the window down and stuck my head out. The rain was as big as pearl tapioca, and a drop smacked me square in the ear.

Strange places like Tonopah, Yesammee, and Simpkins were to the left—and the good pavement went in their direction. At the bottom of the list was Blackwater, and the road that led off that way was a miserable wreckage of old battered islands of macadam in a pathway of cindery gravel. It wound down a channel of huge live oaks, wet and dark. I wondered why I hadn't tried for a nice flight instructing job somewhere in my own part of Pennsylvania where a thunderstorm was impersonal and not this shrieking monster that was daring me to push on through the swamp.

A lumpy mile later, something flew out of the darkness

and flattened itself against the windshield. I let out a sort of "Yowf!", jammed the brakes, and stalled the car.

I climbed out on legs that were rubbery because of driving all that distance with only a couple of cheeseburger stops. No, that wasn't the whole reason. I was plain shaken up by all this, and I was mad at myself for feeling that way. The thing that had plastered itself across the windshield was nothing more frightening than a big swatch of gray Spanish moss.

"You're dumb to let this get to you," I told myself. "A storm's a storm and a swamp's a swamp. That's all there is to it." Of course, it wasn't going to be long before I found out that there really was a heck of a lot more to be shook up about down here. But I didn't know that the first day. I untangled the spongy Spanish moss tendrils from the windshield wiper and tossed the stuff away in the wind.

The car wouldn't start. It growled, coughed, and quit. Growled, coughed, quit. I got so steamed that I kicked it, right in the heater. That hurt me a lot more than it hurt the car, but on the next try it started. "There, you monster. Don't pull that again."

Now I was talking to cars.

Three wet miles later, the road hardened a little, widened a foot or two, and bounced over a railroad track. The oaks arched up to form a tunnel, and I was in the town of Blackwater. A few houses shone chalky white behind the thick tree trunks when the lightning flamed. Thunder shook the car as I peered around for some small sign of life. Either they went to bed early here, or there had been a power failure. Or there wasn't any electricity in the first place. Here and there, as I cruised slowly down the street, I spotted the orange flicker of candles.

Halfway through the dark little town, another road came

in from the north to "T" into the road I was on. At the intersection, when lightning flared for maybe three whole blinding seconds in a row, I spotted a ramshackle frame building nailed together mostly with Dr. Pepper and Coke signs. Out front, glistening like wet bombs, was a stack of fat watermelons. On the other side of the screen-doored entrance was a battered gas pump and a rack of tires.

I pulled into the gravel parking area in front of the place and waited for another flash and crash. They came before I was ready, but I managed to read the sign over the door anyway: *B. Moultrie's Diner and Gen'l Store.*

I'd stopped there for two reasons. I needed some directions, and behind Mr. Moultrie's sooty windows, I had seen the glow of lanterns. I jumped out of the car, dashed through the rain, my sports shirt and slacks soaking it up like limp blotters, yanked open the flimsy screen door, and nearly busted my whole face against the wooden door behind it. That one was locked.

I pounded on it. "Hey, anybody home? I'm drowning out here!"

I thumped again, and after what seemed a heck of a long time, there was some shuffling around, and the door opened just a crack. The crack let out a warm gust of kerosene smell.

"Who's that?" a suspicious voice said. "Who's out there in all that wet?"

"I'm trying to find Blackwater Airport," I told him.

"The *base?* You lookin' for the base?"

Rain ran off corrugations in the tin roof and straight down my collar. It was cold and I jumped. "Look, I'm tired and wet and generally coming unglued. I need gas, and I'm willing to trade my spare tire for some coffee."

"We're closed."

I tried to put my foot in the door, but the crack wasn't wide enough. "Please, please." It turned into a little pushing contest.

Another voice, this one big and beefy, rumbled out of the murk behind the doorman. "Let him in, Moultrie. Can't keep my mind on business with him yippin' away out there."

The door gave way, and I stumbled into a lantern-lit circle of half a dozen rawboned men sitting around in overalls on rickety chairs and boxes of canned goods. Near the glowing lantern on the meat counter, a huge guy with bare arms as big around as my legs said, "What you want at the base, boy?"

"The base?"

"The base, boy. That's what we call it. Army put it there during the war. Hundreds of soldiers here then. Blackwater could've been a big town. A mighty big town. Then they closed the thing down right after the war, and look what happened. Nothin'. Blackwater's same as it ever was."

Maybe it was the weird lighting, but I was a little confused. "What war?" I asked.

"What w— Shooee!" said a less gigantic man sitting among the canned beans. "You funnin' us, fella?"

"Fella" was better than "boy." I felt that I'd gained half a point.

"Shucks, Ralphie," the first man said. "He's too young to remember anything a-tall. The Great Big War," he said to me. "When we fought the Nazis and Japs. Not them other times with the Ko-reeuns and Veet-nameez. I'm talkin' 'bout when there was big planes out at the base. Hundreds of 'em shook the whole town when they took off. Now there's nothin' there but bracken and skeeters."

"An' them nuts with the little planes, Herm," somebody put in.

"Them nuts," I said, "are what I think I'm looking for. The base is the Blackwater Airport, then?"

"That's it, mistuh. Ain't no airport but that till you get all the way to Barnwell." Herm, the guy with the thigh-sized arms, turned to the wrinkled old gaffer who had let me in to start with. "C'mon, Moultrie. Git the fella some coffee."

My eyes were getting used to the darkness. As Moultrie skittered off into the diner half of the building, I saw that I'd stumbled into nothing apparently more evil than a checker match. It was Ralphie's move, and he squinted at the red and black board laid on a stack of soap-chip cases in the middle of the grocery area.

The coffee Moultrie brought me had a stomach-grabbing smoky taste that I found out later was chickory. But it was hot, and I began to feel a little better. I stood there sipping and dripping and watched the game. I'd thought checkers went out with two-piece windshields, but here were the town fathers of Blackwater, going at it as though the fate of the state hung on Ralphie's three kings.

I edged over to Moultrie. "Where's your phone? I'd better call the airport."

"Phone's out," he grumped, sucking in deep breaths and blowing them out of the corner of his cracked lips. "Went out same time's the lights."

"Then I'd better get out there in person," I said. "They'll wonder what happened to me."

Herm with the huge arms looked up. "Don't high-rate yourself, kid. I doubt they need a gas-up boy. Specially so late in the season."

I set the coffee cup down with a clunk, and everybody's

eyes swung my way. "I'm not here as a 'gas-up boy,' " I said. "I'm here as a pilot."

That didn't strike me as a particularly funny statement, but it broke up the game. There was a lot of leg slapping, wide-jawed yocking, and hooting. I got mad, and they loved it.

"Shoot, kid. Out there is three of the toughest flyin' spray pilots that we ever met. They fair goin' to chew you up and spit you out in a cotton patch befo' breakfast. They don' need no *boys* out there. They playin' a man's game. You jes' don't look man enough to us to play it." Herm turned to the others. "Wait'll he meets up with Burnette, hey? Burnette'll trim his feathers for him."

Well, if you're kind of spindly even though you're tall, and you have corn-colored hair that won't stay down whatever you comb it with, and you know darned well you look like a gangling sixteen-year-old no matter how nineteen-year-old you talk, then you just don't hang around and argue with a bunch of South Carolina dirt farmers who could crush barrels with their forearms.

I gave Moultrie a quarter for the coffee and got no change back, listened to his muttering about the rain while he put five gallons in the tank, then I headed out of town on the north road.

Now that I had almost reached Blackwater Airport, or whatever they called it around here, I began to feel less and less like being here at all. I had the letter from Al Derr in my suitcase, and he had certainly said in black and white that I could have the job. He knew how young I was, how few flying hours I had. When I had answered his ad in the aviation magazine, I'd told the truth. But the closer I got to the old air base, the more I felt as though I had no business

16

being there at all. The talk back at Moultrie's about Burnette, whoever he was, didn't make me feel any better, either.

Suddenly, the road began to glow as though made out of silver. I leaned forward and looked through the top of the windshield at the sky. The storm had washed east, and a nearly full moon had broken through the raggedy clouds.

The town of Blackwater was at the edge of the deep swamp I'd been driving through. Now the woods had given way to open fields. A mist rose out of them like a layer of smoke. It drifted across the road, shimmering in the headlights.

The pavement widened, then split around a weather-battered shack that stood on an island of weeds in the middle of the crumbling blacktop.

I slowed down to read the sign that had fallen off the front of the shanty and now leaned against the wall of the little building. The cutout plywood letters had cracked and curled badly, and some of them were missing altogether. But as my headlights moved past, I could make out: BLACKWATER ARMY AIRFIELD. STOP. SHOW IDENTIFICATION.

So this had been the entrance to the ancient air base. Well, maybe thirty-odd years didn't make it exactly ancient, but the place had been built, used, and abandoned years before I was even born. That made it ancient enough for me.

The road curved among dozens of battered building foundations, like squares of old bones in the moonlight through holes in the mist. The Army had taken the wooden walls and tarpaper roofs somewhere else, but the cement block foundations would stay on and on, laid out in the neat patterns of squadron areas long forgotten.

17

Farther on, I rolled past bigger foundations with hunks of plaster walls still standing here and there, dead white under the moon, the mist curling damp fingers around them. The clammy night didn't carry any sound but the smacking of my tires bouncing across potholes in the old road.

But there was some life here, after all. A quarter of a mile ahead, I saw a light glimmering through the fog. I turned down a grass-tufted street toward it, and a gray hulk in the night became an airplane hangar. Beside it was a block-shaped smaller building—the one with the light. As I pulled into a parking lot, my headlights swept across a line of small planes, dripping wet in the darkness. There were four hump-backed, low-winged Pawnee sprayers and what looked like an old Piper Cub. I parked beside the small building, fought through a swarm of mosquitoes that came out of nowhere as though they'd been waiting for me, and slid through the screen door sideways to leave most of the bugs outside.

The old guy sitting behind a battered desk wore a faded khaki shirt and pants that looked as if they were held together with oil stains. The gray fringe around his sunburned bald spot was curly at the edges and needed a trim badly. His face was as weatherworn as exposed sandstone, and about the same color. But his eyes were steady and bright green in the light of the lantern on the desk. He skewered me with them and croaked, "It had better be pretty tootin' urgent."

I stared at him. "What?"

"The reason for you to bust in here this time of night. First the storm nearly wraps up my airplanes, then the power goes out, now some fool kid gets lost and homes in on me like a moth in the night. Am I gonna have to quit work on these books and show you how to get out of here?"

18

"Wait a minute," I told him. "If you're Al Derr, you asked me here. I'm Stewart."

His jaw dropped a full inch. "I'm Derr, but you can't be Stewart. I don't hire grade-schoolers."

"I can't help how young I look," I said. After Moultrie's gang had worked me over, this kind of reception from Al Derr was making me mad. "You know, I'm beginning to wish I'd never heard of this place," I said, knowing what a stupid thing it was to say. But once I got started, I couldn't seem to stop. "The yokels in town already bent my ear about you people and threatened me with some creep named Burnette. Now you don't even want to recognize the fact that I'm here at all."

Derr's eyes hardened. "If you came here to argue, son, I'm just not in the mood. You can turn right around and drive back home. I've got work to do here and not quite enough time to do it in."

The way he bent over his ledger and picked up his pencil sent a little chill through me. I tried to keep it out of my voice, but some of it came through. "I didn't come to argue, Mr. Derr. I came to fly. At least let me show you I can do that."

He tapped the pencil against his teeth, looked at me forever, then turned to a dark corner of the room. "What do you think, Roy?"

I hadn't noticed the other guy at all, sitting there in the shadows, but when he unwound himself from the metal chair and stood up, I noticed him plenty. He was a good six-feet-four and hard as a tight roll of cattle wire under his green flying jumper. His face was lean, and he had cold blue, deep-set hawk's eyes to go with it. The thin nose slashed long and straight to make an inverted T with his razor slit of a mouth. Thin lips and no smile. He flipped a peanut into his mouth and chewed a minute. He hardly moved his jaw when he spoke, and his voice had all the warmth of a hacksaw cutting pipe.

"I'll test him for you, Al. First off, tomorrow morning." The way he said it made me wish almost anybody else had made the offer.

He looked me up and down the way a Doberman pinscher studies a new bone. "If it means anything," he said sourly, "I'm the creep named Burnette."

2

*Y*OU KNOW, WHEN YOU'VE PUT YOUR FOOT so far in your mouth that you can see the scars on your knee, the best thing to do is shut up. So I shut up.

"You'll find the place we stay at back in Blackwater," Al Derr said. "Turn right when you get to town. It's called Magnolia Cabins. You'll see the sign. Owned by Aunt Agony Anthony. You can get breakfast at Moultrie's and be back here by eight in the morning."

I drove back to gloomy Blackwater, not quite knowing whether I'd been hired or fired or what, and I turned to the right the way they said, and in a minute or so, I spotted a worn wooden sign dripping in the headlights. *Magnolia Cabins. Comfortable Lodging, Weekly Rates. Mrs. Agnes*

Anthony, Prop. I was sure the sign hadn't changed since she must have rented the little faded white clapboard cabins to married officers assigned to the base. There were eight of the little boxes, scattered in the woods behind the big main house.

I pulled into the gravel driveway, climbed the groaning porch steps, and knocked. The door creaked open, and I squinted against the lantern's glare. She was small, chunky, and wore a heavy knit sweater over her raggedy dress. In the wavy shadows of the kerosene lantern, I got the idea that Mrs. Agnes Anthony was a little older than Fort Sumter, but she turned out to be somewhere in her fifties.

"I'm Greg Stewart," I told her. "They told me out at the airport that you have a room."

She gave me the kind of look you save for unusual beetles and said, "Al Derr sent you? You don't look like a pilot."

"Well, I am, whether anybody around here thinks so or not. And I'm tired, and I hope you've—"

"Now, hold on there, son. I've got a cabin for you. No use getting in a swivet over nothing." With her free hand, she clutched her sweater tighter around her barrel-shaped body. "Mercy, you'd think a body wouldn't shiver so in the Deep South. If I'd known there'd be nights like this, I'd never have left Vermont. At least there 'twas honest cold, not sneaky, clammy cold like this."

"When did you come down here?"

"Nineteen-ought-forty-two," she said. "Me and poor Tod Anthony. Just two lonesome Yankees here in peanut and cotton country, trying to make an honest dollar. Opened these cabins the same year. I did the managing, and Tod did the carpentering, fixing, painting, lawn work, clearing, grubbing, and other odd jobs, but all the time fooling with that camera of his. Should have paid more attention to the cabin business, and we would have made more of a go of it."

We walked toward the gloomy cabin she had pointed out. "Is he still . . . I noticed on your sign, it just says—"

"Him!" she snorted. "Two years after we got started here, Tod went over to Moultrie's for a bag of flour one afternoon, and I haven't seen him since. Not since. He didn't get off scot-free, though. Not by a long shot. Still has to send me a support check every month like clockwork or I have the law right on him. Yessiree."

She flipped up the collar of her heavy sweater and snorted. I wasn't so sure I blamed Old Man Anthony for taking such a long time to bring back that flour, and I could see why the guys at the base called her Aunt Agony.

The cabin had a rickety iron bed, a chest of drawers out of a 1930 late-late show, a chair that almost begged not to be sat on too often, and the smell of an old attic. "Bath's there," she announced, pointing at a door in the far corner. "Each cabin's got its own since I took over. Before then, it was a room and a path." She joggled up and down in silent laughter, and I tossed my suitcase on the bed.

"Did you say you worked at the base?" she said with sudden sharpness.

"I'm taking a flight test for it tomorrow."

She raised her thin eyebrows in the lantern light. "With who?"

"With Burnette."

She stuck her hand out, palm up. "'In that case, I got to be paid in advance."

"For the whole season?"

"Oh, no," she said. "Just for the one night. You did say Burnette."

23

At that point, the bare bulb in the cabin ceiling glared into blinding life. The power line break had been fixed, but I wished it hadn't. Mrs. Anthony might better have sent her husband out for paint instead of flour. I doubted that the place had ever felt a brush.

Sleep just wouldn't come that night. I killed seven mosquitoes; then some bug crawled across my neck and sent me straight up into the dead air. It was a green fly. I never was able to swat it, even with a rolled-up pair of pants. It was perched on the back of the chair looking at me when I opened a fuzzy eye sometime after dawn. I got up, dressed in soggy dungarees, and drove down the silent street to Moultrie's.

The checker game had long since folded, and Moultrie was shuffling around the grocery store, putting things back in what he considered order. He came into the diner section when I sat down at the warped wooden counter. The raunchy coffee cost a quarter in the morning, too.

"Heer'd you was takin' a flight test this mornin'," the old man said.

I looked up from the cracked cup. "News moves around in this town."

"Don't have far to go." He leaned against the counter, taking in wheezy breaths and blowing them back out the side of his mouth. "Burnette, huh."

"What about him?"

"Heer'd he's givin' you the test. Too bad. He's tough as a skunk. And a little strange, too, if you was to ask me."

I swirled the last of the coffee around the bottom of the cup. "All right, I'm asking."

"Well, standoffish, you know? Don't really associate with the other boys out there. And every time he gits a chance, he just disappears."

"Who wouldn't?" I said. "What's here in Blackwater?"

"No, I mean *really* disappears. He never goes with none of the others to Columbia or Charleston, or anywhere else they know of. Just takes one of the planes and flies off somewhere by himself. Somethin' odd 'bout Roy Burnette."

Moultrie was obviously the town gossip—or one of them —but I couldn't get what he'd said about Burnette out of my mind. I drove slowly to the base through the first heat of the morning, dreading what was going to happen next. "You've got more than two hundred hours," I told myself. "You know how to make an airplane talk. You've got the touch." That's what they'd told me back at the Clark Ridge Airport, anyway. But I wished my old instructor was here to tell me again. Especially when I saw Roy Burnette leaning against the door jamb of the little administration shack as friendly as a cattle prod and looking as if he'd just swallowed a potful of the worst chickory Moultrie had ever boiled over. He flipped a peanut into his razor slit of a mouth and hitched his head toward the beige-and-red plane that I had thought was an aged Piper Cub.

As we walked closer, I could see I was wrong about that. It was a lot like the old Cub with its two seats, one behind the other, narrow fuselage, high wing, and little donut wheels. But it had flaps and an oversized engine. It was a Cub's grandson, officially known in the trade as a Super Cub.

"Front seat," Burnette ordered, unknotting the tie-down ropes. I buckled the seat belt, and he folded into the little seat behind me. "Shoulder straps, too, Stewart. This isn't a pleasure hop. Let's go."

I pumped the primer, opened the throttle a crack, and turned the key. The propeller ground around a couple of times, then the engine caught. I eased off the heel brakes.

We taxied across the wide, crumbling apron, jounced through a weedy area, and turned onto a runway that was wider and longer than any I had ever seen. It was cracked pretty badly, and here and there weeds and grass had taken root. But it was so huge that there were plenty of usable stretches left for a small plane.

"Take off," Burnette said in my ear over the engine's mumble.

The little yellow wind sock on the hangar showed no wind at all. I checked the magnetos, then booted the rudder, and we scudded down the endless runway.

The Super Cub was off the ground before I was even half ready, something like an express elevator at full boost. I leveled off much too fast and put air between me and the seat. I realized with a twinge that Burnette was floating against his belt, too.

He tapped my shoulder and leaned close. "I'll take it."

We flew east about half a mile, made a nice lazy swing, and headed back toward the old air base. To the left, the white squares of abandoned building foundations stretched away to the distant tumbledown entrance gate and the narrow black strip that was the road south to Blackwater. On the other side of the broad macadam runway, the forest and underbrush had taken back a lot of the land the Army Air Force had cleared in the 1940's. The heavy growth had almost made it to the swampy north side of the runway, and at both ends of the paved strip, jack pines and weed trees had grown into twenty-foot-high green barriers.

Then the engine howled as the little plane skittered around, almost pivoting on a wing tip and gluing me tight in the seat. The nose plunged and the ground rushed toward us. We leveled out inches above the trees and rocketed toward the runway. The woods fell away. Burnette

26

jammed the nose down. The pavement leaped at us. We flared out with the weed tufts snapping the wheels at a hundred miles an hour.

My stomach rolled over. The pines at the runway's far end teetered toward us, growing fast, their furry branches waiting to bat us out of the air. Burnette rammed the throttle home. The plane vaulted out of the clearing, and the base fell away behind us.

We flattened out at 150 feet, flipped steeply left, then slammed around the other way, whirling on a wing tip. We skidded tightly and came out of it lined up precisely on the runway, heading west.

They just plain didn't fly that way at Clark Ridge.

"Try it," Burnette rapped.

My hands were wet and shaking as I grabbed the stick and throttle. Burnette had to be some kind of bird-beaked kook. Nobody could fly like this and expect to survive to be even a gray-haired twenty-five.

The Super Cub arrowed back over the trees before I was ready. I jammed the nose down too late and too far. There was an immediate tug on the stick from the rear. The nose came up.

"Do that with a full load of defoliant spray, and you're dead," Burnette snarled in my ear.

I nosed the plane down more carefully, held it there, and powered it in over the edge of the woods. I inched back the stick and held the wheels a foot off the runway almost to the end, rammed in power, and we clawed out of there over the trees with barely ten feet between us and disaster. Too close. Too darned close.

But Burnette said, "Fair. Not good, just fair. Drag her in with the engine and plunk her down just past the trees."

That wasn't so easy, either. The pines reached for us.

27

I dropped the flaps, hung the little plane on its propeller, and mushed in tail-low. The prop wash swished through the treetops. I chopped power. We hit hard and barely rolled fifty feet. "Taxi her in," Burnette said.

Al Derr waited for us back at the tie-down line. "Well?" he asked Burnette as we finished roping the wing struts and tail to the iron loops set in the apron pavement.

Burnette emptied a cellophane bag of salted peanuts into his palm and tossed one into his mouth. "No question about where he learned to fly. These eastern guys all handle it the same. Safe and smooth. High and nine lives above stalling speed. Only trouble is, you just can't spread cotton defoliant that way and make money for the company."

The warm morning had just turned chilly. Maybe my dad was right, after all. I was too young and inexperienced for what they wanted me to do. And they knew it. I should have stayed in Clark Ridge a year or two until I got more hours in my logbook.

"You know I'd rather have a steady ex-military guy with some light-plane time," Derr said. He kicked at a dandelion growing right in the apron pavement. "Only trouble is, the kid here is the only applicant I got this late in the season." He flicked a grasshopper off his sleeve and scratched his shoulder thoughtfully. Then he surprised all the wind out of me. "What I said last night wasn't quite true. We need you, I'm afraid," he said. "We'll take you on. Got to."

That wasn't the way I'd dreamed of being hired, but it sure beat no job at all.

"Come into the office for a few minutes; then Roy'll brief you on the Pawnee. First, we got some paperwork to do on you, and I've got a little briefing of my own."

Through the next hour, we got all the forms signed, the

28

Social Security and insurance organized; then I found out more about an entirely new kind of flying than I had thought was possible in that short a time. Although I was to get a low-flying waiver, there still were plenty of restrictions. Al Derr ticked them off and told me I'd better remember them, or else. "We run a clean operation here, Stewart. If somebody goofs up, we don't even check it out with home base in Illinois. We just dump him fast."

I learned a lot in those few minutes with Al Derr. He told me that he and Roy Burnette, two other pilots, a pair of mechanics, and a loading boss came down here to South Carolina every summer. "We start the season with Veronica Agricultural Flying Service's home office in Illinois. Then we come down here for defoliation contracts with the cotton farmers around Blackwater."

I asked him if all the worry about insecticides wasn't hurting the agricultural flying business in general.

"Sure, but we change every time we find better ways to do things. We're using only insecticides that have a short life. No more DDT—that seems to stay around much longer than anyone had ever expected. Now we're using more stuff like chlordane, which loses its strength and disintegrates fast. No residual. Same with the defoliants."

He plowed through the papers on his desk, found a folder, and handed it to me. "Here's the scoop on the stuff we use on the cotton. It's a leaf killer, not an insecticide. Makes the leaves fall off the cotton plants, and then the cotton bolls are exposed so the mechanical picker can get at them. That saves the cotton farmers whole days of extra work, and they can use every saving they can get. Cotton used to be *the* business down here, but nylon and rayon and other synthetic fabrics have made it a tougher way to make a buck every year. A lot of the farmers are changing to soy beans and other crops. I guess it won't be long before our cotton defoliation business has to turn into something else, too."

He switched the subject abruptly, maybe trying to catch me off guard. "O.K., one more time. What are the three cardinal rules?"

"One, no spraying when the wind is over six miles an hour," I said. "Two, make spraying passes crosswind and turnarounds into the wind. Three, where you can't avoid a hill, make one-way passes away from the hill, not toward it. And"—I threw in for good measure—"keep the safety straps tight, and remember that stalls happen fast in tight turns."

Al stuck out his bottom lip and nodded thoughtfully. "Good enough, Stewart. Just keep remembering it all. Now I want to give you a rundown on the people here. I'm head of the unit, and Roy is chief pilot. Under him, we got Eddie Pelton from New Jersey—he got his experience spraying the Jersey swamps for mosquito control—and Carl Davis. Carl put in a few years on California tomatoes and artichokes before he came to us. And, of course, the fourth pilot is going to be you. You're replacing a fella who left us last week to fly with an airline in South America. He'd been waiting six months for the job, and it finally came through."

Al gazed through the cloudy office window at the dark woods across the runway. "That's one of the troubles with ag flying. Hard to make a real career of it. Got to follow the crops all over the country to make any money. It's a tough life. A tough . . . well, anyway"—he brought himself back to the business at hand—"we got two mechanics, Frank Kingston and Harry Feather, and a loading chief, Dobbs Musserman. That fills out the roster. Just eight of us to handle all the cotton that's left in this area. And just a couple of weeks to do it in. Eddie and Carl have been spraying since daylight this morning. Roy would be, too, except that today he's breaking you in."

Al circled around behind his desk and plopped into the creaky chair. "That about sums it up, kid. You got any questions?"

I shouldn't have asked it, I guess, but I had to. "Just one, I think. I know I'm all you could get on short notice, and I know that Roy thinks I'm still wearing pinfeathers. And I'm sorry I busted in here last night with a fat chip on my shoulder. But that hardly seems enough for Roy to hate me. What's with that guy?"

Al looked at me in silence too long, and I began to fidget with the folder he'd given me. "Roy's a heck of a good man," he finally said, but he said it very carefully.

"He sure tries to cover it up. He acts like he's got a grudge against the world."

And then Al said something that I knew slipped out without his wanting it to. "He's had it tough for about thirty years. One lousy break, and—" Al's face was suddenly as red as Herm's huge forearms back in last night's lantern light at Moultrie's. "Forget it, kid. He's the best ag pilot I ever ran into. And I've been in the business a long time. You couldn't have a better teacher."

Twenty minutes later, Roy, sour as a green crabapple, had told me all about the Piper Pawnee, rap-rap-rap, one fast fact after another. If I hadn't had a pretty quick memory, I would have been lost. I think he was still testing me.

I got into the single-seat low-winged white sprayer around ten o'clock. I could hardly wait to get up in the air by myself. The Pawnee seemed like a great little ship, enclosed cockpit set high and about halfway back from the nose; struts reinforcing the wings for quick high-G pullouts; metal

31

propeller to cut through stray wires; and a big six-cylinder Lycoming with 260 horses.

I ducked through the window entrance to the small cockpit and nearly sat on a bright red plastic safety helmet. "Put that on," Roy ordered, "and wear it every time you work."

When I'd finally gotten myself arranged and everything was tight, Roy crouched on the wing walk beside me.

"Take her up to a thousand feet and see how she handles; then make some spraying passes along the runway. I want to see you wet down every foot of it, six gallons per minute."

"Wet it down? With what?"

"With water," Roy snapped. "We've just pumped a thousand pounds of it into the hopper."

I gave the primer a couple of shots, pushed the mixture control to full rich, and set the throttle open a crack. Then I hit the starter button. She flipped over and caught with a smooth *vvvmmm*. Roy stepped down from the wing, and I let off the brakes.

I let them off too fast, and I had opened the throttle too far. The tail swung around before I could catch it. I felt a solid thud.

Roy picked himself up, wearing an expression that would have made Attila the Hun shudder.

"I'm sorry—" I began lamely.

His arm shot into the cockpit and grabbed a handful of my shirt. He shook me like a rattle and stuck a jaw the size of a bulldozer blade in my face. *"You want to play games, you play somewhere else! Not with me!"*

"I . . . it was . . . an . . . accident." My teeth were clacking.

"Pull that lever!" Roy shouted.

"What?"

He let me go and slapped the hopper handle. "Open it. All the way."

"But that—"

"OPEN IT!" he roared.

I opened it. Water poured out of the hopper, flooding the ramp around the plane.

"Count to thirty. Slow."

I counted.

"That's enough. Close it."

I closed it.

"All right, joker. Now you fill up the tank again."

"Where's the hose?" I asked.

"No hose. You're going to use a three-gallon bucket. Cut the switch, leave the plane right here, and walk."

I walked. Twenty-one long trips between the Pawnee and the spigot near the hanger. Water weighs eight pounds per gallon. The twenty-four-pound return trip felt like three times that at the end of the hour it took to fill up the hopper again.

Through it all, Roy leaned against the Pawnee's fuselage, slowly chewing salted peanuts. If Al Derr had appeared or if anyone at all had come out of the hanger to check into this crazy business, I might have felt that I could put up a kick.

But if anyone noticed what was going on between Roy and me, he kept his nose out of it. So what could I do? I wanted the job, so I carried the water. And I sweated. And I hated Roy more with every bucketful.

"If I ever get the hint of a chance to get even with him," I swore to myself, "look out, Roy Burnette."

The cavern-sized hopper in front of the cockpit was finally refilled. I dropped the pail and glared at Roy.

"Get in," he said. "Start it. Get out of here carefully this time. And grow up some."

I forced the hot anger back until I could do something about it. The Pawnee was easy to taxi straight ahead, even though it sat on conventional main gear and a tail wheel. The fuselage sloped down toward the long nose, and visibility was great.

I took her way down to the end of the runway. I didn't know how a thousand pounds of cargo would make the plane react, and I was taking no chances.

Everything checked out fine. I swung her into the light breeze and fed in the gas.

The sprayer roared forward. I got the tail up, and she lifted free of the runway, climbing fast, even though the nose was below the horizon. That was one of the unusual things about the Pawnee—made you feel as though you were going straight up while you seemed to sit dead level.

When the altimeter needle hit a thousand, I flattened her out and pushed the little plane through stalls, turns, stalls out of turns—a whole string of maneuvers—until I felt that I knew her well enough not to be taken by surprise.

Then I throttled back, dropped the long nose, and let her sink toward the base. I came in fast and flared out low, just past the pines at the east end. My left hand was wrapped around the tank gate valve handle. I thumbed down the release button on the top of the handle and pushed the lever forward, opposite the "6" mark on its quadrant. Water jetted from the nozzles along the spray booms below the trailing edge of each wing. It settled to the runway behind me like fine whirling rain.

Near the end of the pass, I flipped the valve handle back, poured on the coal, and we howled out of there. I made what I thought was a good turnaround and laid another dark swath of water along the runway beside the first.

It took nearly twenty minutes to empty the tank. By that time, I knew I was getting pretty good. When I cut the throttle, dropped the flaps, and brought her in right opposite the old hanger, I expected some kind of recognition from Roy. Not a pat on the head or a lollipop. Maybe just a nod. But what I got was a good chewing out. He had picked out all the little flaws in my very first flight in that Pawnee, and he threw them back at me like bullets.

"You over-controlled on the third pull-up . . . used too much rudder on your turn recoveries . . . shut off the spray too soon four times . . . came in too flat to start with, too steep after that . . . "

It was a grade A personality clash, or whatever the fancy name is for two guys who can't stand each other at first sight. While I stood there, pale as bread dough and trying to stop the angry shakes, I swore again I'd get back at Roy Burnette. It was a fool way to react, but one way or another, I was going to get even with him. Of course, that was before I found out about the trouble he was in.

3

*H*AVE YOU EVER STRUGGLED TO GET YOUR-
self into something, then found out that the people who
warned you against it were probably right all along? That
describes my first few days with the South Carolina con-
tingent of the Veronica Agricultural Flying Service. My flying was all over the sky. I couldn't find my target fields
after turnarounds. I actually bounced off one cotton patch
on a late flare-out. I was afraid Eddie Pelton and Carl Davis
would begin to call me the beast with ten thumbs.

"Know what you're doing, Greg?" Eddie said at Moultrie's after I'd had a particularly bad afternoon sharing a
big job with him ten miles west of Blackwater. "You're try-

ing too hard. Relax a little—not much, or a big turpentine pine will bat you right out of the sky. But quit tensing up. You're a good-enough pilot not to pull that."

I'd gotten to like Eddie. He was a stumpy little bald guy. His sunburned forehead came up to my shoulders, but his arms were about four inches longer than mine. He had the adjustable seat in his Pawnee jacked up to its highest notch.

"The guy's all helmet and arms," Dobbs Musserman, the loading chief, had said to me one morning after Eddie had climbed into his sprayer. I liked Dobbs, too. He was as tough as a cinder block with a face like old cowhide. A dead cigar was part of his battered uniform. The rest of it was a dusty suit of blue denims. He never said much to Len, his gawky, black, teen-aged, part-time helper, but they worked together fine, pumping loads of defoliant from the tank truck into our hoppers so quickly that most of the time Eddie and I just stayed in the cockpit between runs.

I swallowed a mouthful of Moultrie's coffee. It was just as bad as ever. I couldn't seem to build up an immunity. "You're right," I told Eddie. "I've been as shaky as a one-bladed propeller. I think Roy did that to me. I'm glad he got sent out with Carl Davis. What's with that guy?"

"Roy's a heck of a good pilot. Best Veronica's got."

"I know he's good, but why does he hate everybody? Only guy he seems to get along with is Al Derr."

"Guess he believes that old military business about the more your men like you, the less discipline you've got. I listen to what he tells me about flying and steer clear of him otherwise."

"Was Roy in the service?" I asked.

"Air Force."

"When? Korea? Viet Nam?" Roy was affecting me like

a rattlesnake. You're scared of the darned thing, but you want to find out more about it.

Eddie laughed. "Come on, Greg. Just 'cause you weren't born then doesn't mean World War II is ancient history. Roy was in the 'Brown Shoe Air Force'—the Army Air Corps. He was a service pilot. 'Snake pilots,' they called them, because their pilot badge had an S on the shield. They flew all kinds of odd-ball missions, from target towing to flying for the British general staff. *I'm* the guy who flew in Korea. And Carl Davis has been a civil pilot for twenty years."

I bit into a lumpy donut, then talked around it. "That's all you know about Roy after flying with him for two seasons?"

"He doesn't talk much about himself."

Beyond the pass-through window behind the counter, we watched Moultrie suck-and-blow his wheezes back in the grimy kitchen. Then Eddie said, "Seems to me that I heard Roy had started out in combat crew training on bombers and then ended up as a snake pilot. Something must have happened in between. In fact, I think once he said he took his combat crew training right around here somewhere. On B-24's."

Revenge isn't the healthiest idea to get hooked on, but I was still enough of a kid to think that I owed Roy something unpleasant for the way he had treated me. Al Derr had given me the first clue that something had happened to Roy in the past that still bothered him. Now Eddie Pelton had filled in a little more of Roy's background.

I gazed into my coffee mug. Al had said Roy's troubles began thirty years ago. That would make it World War II. Interesting. And, according to Eddie, Roy had started out to be a bomber pilot, then had switched to something else.

What could that mean? Much as I had it in for Roy, I couldn't believe that he would have ducked combat.

Eddie was through talking about the subject of Roy Burnette, so I tried another angle later in the day. An unexpected one, as a matter of fact. Aunt Agony Anthony actually asked me to join her on the front porch of the main house for lemonade. Can you imagine a rough, tough sprayer pilot like me swigging lemonade with that old gal on her broken front stoop? Well, it wasn't bad; a lot better than Moultrie's boiled chickory.

We sat there rocking in her squeaky high-backed wicker chairs, watching night close in around us. I felt like a little kid visiting his grandmother.

"It sure isn't like the wild old days," she said. "About this time, you'd hear the engines revving up at the base for night training. Then pretty soon, they'd come roaring up over Blackwater, fair shaking the roofs off."

"Big planes?"

"Four-engine ones. B-something."

"B-24's?"

"That's it. B-24's. Fat bodies, thin wings. And noise? Oh, it was something!"

"Was Blackwater really much of a training base?" I took a sip of tart lemonade. "There's only one runway out there. Looks more like some kind of auxiliary field."

"Well, that's exactly right. The big fields were at Charleston and Savannah, and they used Blackwater for cross-country stops and special training. Gave them practice at using smaller airports. The boys didn't much like flying out of here, though. Not after the jinx story got started."

"Jinx? What kind of jinx?"

"Oh, shoot, wasn't no more'n a silly superstition. A few of the planes that took off from here just disappeared.

Never were seen again. That kind of unsettled everybody for a while. Some pilots are as superstitious as sailors, you know. Say, I have a few pictures inside that Tod took out there if you want to look at them sometime."

I thanked her, but now I was too busy concocting a theory of sorts: Roy Burnette was probably sent to Charleston or Savannah for combat crew training. There, he got out of combat training, and ever since he has been haunted by whatever it was that had happened—probably it was the reason he was made a service pilot instead of a bomber man.

"Come on now, smart guy," I told myself back in my hot oven of a cabin. "What kind of nothing story is that? You're as bad as those guys who she said believed in a stupid jinx."

The next morning, it turned out that I didn't have time to worry it further. I slapped the alarm clock, dressed fast, and drove through the sticky darkness to Moultrie's. It was 5:30 A.M.

Carl Davis had flown back in last night from somewhere near Florence, and he was hanging pouch-eyed over eggs fried as tough as bathing caps. "Mornin'," he mumbled. "Pull up a stool, and we'll get poisoned together."

Carl wasn't a bad guy. A couple of years younger than Roy, he was built like a Western dirt farmer—thin hips, wide shoulders, big hands. He had blond hair that was thinning out, but he wore it long enough to hang over his forehead. His watery blue eyes were in a permanent squint from too much flying without sunglasses.

"Did Roy come back with you?" I asked as casually as I could.

"Yep. He's got a day off coming, and he wanted to get back here and borrow the Super Cub. He's spraying a spread near yours this morning; then he shoves off this afternoon."

Moultrie set my burned toast on the counter with a clank.

"Where the heck does Roy go on those mysterious trips of his?" I asked Carl.

"Dunno. Don't care. His business, not mine."

I gathered from his tone that he'd been interested once himself, then got told to butt out in no uncertain terms. Was I reading too much into a few growled words, or were they all a little afraid of Roy?

"Where are you flying today, kid?"

"Hinkle Farm. Five miles east."

"Umm," Carl said. "I know that one. Bad deal. Gotta watch yourself every minute." He dropped some coins on the counter. "Gotta get moving. See you, Greg."

As the screen door clapped behind him, the Blackwater freight agent came in and tossed down a cup of coffee without even wincing. Maybe he'd never had the real thing. "You one of them sprayer pilots, ain't you?" he asked me. "Going to see Roy Burnette today? Tell him he's got a crate down at the station. Come in last night. Asked me to tell him direct, but heck, if you're going to see him, he'll get the word quicker this way."

Hinkle's layout was mainly a three-hundred-acre cotton field carved out of the woods, bounded with trees—not just on one side or two sides. No, this little gem had nice tall oaks and buttonwoods on all four sides. Tucked almost out of sight halfway along the west edge was the Hinkle house and barn.

When I landed a mile or so away on the straight stretch of dirt road both Roy and I were to use as a loading strip, Roy's Pawnee was already parked beside Dobbs Musser-

41

man's loading truck. I pulled up near them, cut the switch, and walked over to Roy. He nodded and turned back to the pumping operation.

"Freight agent in Blackwater wants me to tell you a crate came in for you last night."

That took care of my message-carrying chore, and I reached down for a stalk of grass to chew on. When I came back up, Roy was standing right over me.

"What makes you so interested in my personal business?" he rapped. "I asked that guy to keep his mouth shut about that shipment."

"My gosh, I'm only doing you a favor. Get off my back, will you?"

He gave me a look somewhere between a sneer and a snarl—a snerl. Then he scruffed back through road dust to his own plane. I found myself interested in what might be in that crate back in the Blackwater railroad station.

Roy took off for his own assignment about two miles east, and I pulled up to the truck as the dust of his take-off swirled away into the roadside weeds. Dobbs and I listened to his engine fading as skinny Len began to pump the chemicals into my Pawnee's hopper.

"Real pilot, that Roy," Dobbs Musserman said, his big blue jaw working around his ragged cigar. "Don't come any better."

"So everybody keeps telling me," I grumped. "Well, I'd better get at it. Don't want to hold up the party or Roy'll have to help me finish my part of the work, and that will mess up his afternoon off."

Dobbs reached into the cockpit to lay fingers like sausages on my arm. "You'd better get a tighter grip on yourself, kid, before you take on that field of Hinkle's. That's a tough assignment. Those are big trees around that field of his. You don't want to barrel in there with a mad on like you got for Roy. Calm down some."

I answered him by jabbing the starter button, and I climbed off the road fast, bending toward Hinkle's before I was fifty feet up. I spotted my raggedy-shirted flagboy along the south edge of the acreage, dropped in over the east end, and shoved the hopper valve open. Roy Burnette! He treated me like a high school freshman just because I'd gotten off on the wrong foot.

I whipped back and forth across that field, so quick on the turnarounds that my panting flagboy barely had time to scamper sideways after each pass and raise his white marker pole to line up for the next swath.

I'll admit that Dobbs Musserman had a point. Maybe if I'd been less worked up over Roy's attitude toward me and had been paying more attention to what I was doing, I wouldn't have gotten into trouble so fast. When I saw that little black dot against the trees at the far end of the field, I might have remembered my old instructor's rule-of-thumb. It goes about like this: When something just stays in the same relative position through your windshield, when it doesn't move up or down, right or left, then you're going to hit it.

What I saw was a bird, about a quarter of a mile away, flapping lazily across Hinkle's cotton field. It simply stayed in the same spot through the cockpit plexiglass and got bigger.

And I hunched over the control stick and hopper valve handle, feeling sorry for myself, roaring four feet above the cotton at 105 miles per hour toward the flagboy. By the time I realized the big bird and I were on collision courses, he was close enough for me to count feathers. He was a buzzard about the size of a flying Volkswagen. His head swung my way just as I decided I had to do something fast. I'm sure his beak dropped open in amazement. He tried to flap up and away, but by now he was floundering through the air dead ahead and growing huge!

I had one place to go. Under him. I chopped the power and ducked. The Pawnee's wheels made a frothy salad out of the cotton bolls and plant tops. Just ahead, the flagboy heaved his pole aside and scrambled hard for a neutral corner.

I missed the buzzard. But now I had another problem. I sure couldn't go under my flagboy. I poured in the power, but the heavy cotton plants hung onto the wheels an instant too long. Three feet off the ground, I had to swerve to the left to miss the guy.

I could see it coming. I jerked the throttle back all the way. The engine died and backfired just as the left wingtip dug into the soft ground. The Pawnee leaped sideways, throwing me against the safety straps. My helmet clanged against the cockpit canopy. My ears rang like school bells. The sprayer's right wing tore through the cotton. A spray of shredded green and white fluff burst across the canopy. The plane cartwheeled and jackrabbitted to a stop. It was still on its feet, but we were both aching.

The final lurch threw me hard into the side of the cockpit. If it hadn't been for the helmet, I think my flying days would have been over right there. As it was, the blow turned things a fuzzy silent gray. I didn't come out of it until two huge hands ripped open the canopy and hauled me out on the wing.

"You all right, boy?" a strangely familiar voice rasped in my ear. I forced an eye open and stared up at the beefy face blotting out the sky above me. It was Huge-Arms Herm

44

of the Moultrie checker game crowd. Then I realized that Herm was Herm Hinkle. This was his field.

The moan of the loading truck told me that Dobbs had seen me go down. I sat up and watched the truck plow through the sea of ripe cotton. Roy was with Dobbs; he must have been loading up when they heard me hit.

"How is he?" Dobbs shouted as they leaped out of the cab.

"Seems O.K. Mite dazed. Take a look at the flagboy."

Roy trotted toward me, and Dobbs called out, "I think the flagboy sprained his ankle."

Roy stood over me, looming against the bright sky like a giant angry statue. Roy the Righteous. "Swell," he snapped. "Just swell. Mopping up this mess wipes out everybody's afternoon."

I wobbled up out of the cotton and raised a forefinger. "Just a minute. There was this buzzard. Bigger than a bread-board . . . box . . ." I looked down and found that I wasn't standing any more. I was on my knees. Then the ground came up and shoved against my face, and it felt fine.

"Concussion," I heard Roy say way up in the sky above me. "You know, Dobbs, this might just be one of my worst days since 1944."

Forty-four. The number and I slid down a long quiet chute together. I was to discover within a few hours that it was a magic number. It opened doors to the past.

Roy and Dobbs weren't nearly as casual as I thought they were being, of course. After I folded in the dirt between cotton rows, they raced me and the flagboy into Blackwater in the truck. Doc Winfell interrupted his breakfast of bacon and grits to agree with Roy that I did indeed have a mild concussion. We left the freckle-faced flagboy in Doc's living room office to have his ankle taped, and Roy and Dobbs took me to my cabin at Aunt Agony's.

"Doc said rest until tomorrow, so do it," Roy said. "Then you can begin the paperwork with Al."

"Fired?" I was still pretty fuzzy.

"Don't know, Stewart," Roy said as he left the cabin. "That was an $18,000 airplane you bounced around that field."

Dobbs stuck his head back in as they left. "I'll have your flagboy talk about it with Al, kid. He saw the whole thing. Get some rest."

It took a lot of talk, not just from the flagboy, and a lot of forms. But by late afternoon the next day, Al Derr came to the conclusion that I had done the best I could, once I noticed the buzzard. What he was decent enough not to say was that I should have noticed it a lot sooner.

The plane had been trucked back to the base, and lights were going to burn late in the old hangar. Tall, crow-like Frank Kingston and bullet-headed, stumpy Harry Feather sure weren't going to lose any love on me. I stayed out of there the rest of the day.

In fact, I didn't get back to the base for two more days. When I did, I knew a lot more about Roy. It began with a late evening phone call from Al Derr.

"You feeling O.K., Greg? I was going to suggest that you take one more day off anyway, but we've just got word there's a warm front coming through here in the morning. It'll put us out of action for about forty-eight hours. You got any personal business, now's the time. I'll see you and the other pilots on Friday."

That was just what I needed because an idea had hit me and I needed a free day to work it out. The rain began in the clammy hours before daylight. I dressed to its patter on the cabin roof. My khakis were damp, and so was the car's upholstery. I was on the road out of town while it was still dark. When a feeble dawn finally came, I was twenty miles on the way to Charleston and having real coffee in a real restaurant on Route 17.

I cut into a stack of wheatcakes and wondered if I was kidding myself. What I had to go on was a big fat guess. Roy's comment back in the cotton field was the last link in what I hoped was a chain of clues. To me, it added up this way: He had trained around here, and whatever had happened—if it was big enough—should be in the papers of the nearest large city. That was Charleston. I'd thought of trying a search of newspaper files a few days ago, but going through maybe three years of old newspapers would have been a bigger job than I had time for. It would have meant leafing through nearly a thousand daily papers, page by page. But yesterday, Roy himself had cut the figure by two-thirds. ". . . one of my worst days since 1944," he had said.

All I had to do now was check the papers for that one year.

4

$\mathcal{T}$HE DRIZZLE WENT WITH ME ALL THE WAY down Route 17. I smacked along wet blacktop through Snuggedy, hit four lanes leading into the western edge of Charleston, then crossed the divided bridge over the Ashby River into downtown. With only one wrong turn and the help of a police officer under a yellow slicker, I found the *Southeastern Advocate* building before nine-thirty.

"You want the 'Morgue'?" a short blond girl in a floppy orange sweater asked me with a grin. "Honey, nobody's called it that for fifteen years. You mean the Reference Library."

It was on the second floor, down a corridor between rows of tiny fluorescent-lighted busy cubicles.

"Nineteen forty-four," the tall, precise, gray lady-in-charge said, more or less to herself. "Should be about"—she ran a long forefinger across the spines of endless hardcover-bound newspapers—"here."

She slipped the clumsy dark green volume out of its slot on the low shelf and clumped it on a reading table.

"Just sign the register, and you can begin with this one. January 1 to March 31, 1944. The rest of the year is in the next three volumes."

I thanked her, edged into the straight-back chair, and began turning the crackly old pages.

Names that had been only words in history classes back in Clark Ridge seemed to be alive here in this musty little file room in Charleston. General Dwight Eisenhower, in England to direct the invasion of Europe, was explaining the Allied campaign in Italy. In late February, one thousand RAF bombers left Berlin in flames. In South Carolina, combat crew training went on hot and heavy . . . but routine.

I got the second file book. In May, the Germans along the French Coast went on a rabbit hunt. They were afraid that rabbits running into their defensive mine fields would set them off early. In Washington, the Navy announced that half its personnel in that city were women—something called WAVES.

I turned a page, and the headlines jumped at me: ALLIES INVADE EUROPE. I'd gotten to June 6. Now the paper was jammed with invasion news, and local items were shoved farther into each edition.

By noon, I'd gone through almost two hundred editions of the *Southeastern Advocate*. The paper was brittle, and I had to hold each page straight as I turned it. My arms were tired and my neck was stiff. And I had found absolutely nothing about Roy Burnette.

I slid the book back in place and walked out of there. The idea had been stupid. In the same block, I found a coffee shop and ordered a cheeseburger and coffee. That made me feel better, though the rain still pelted down outside. I stared through the restaurant window at the slow traffic on Cannon Street.

Roy *had* said 1944. I *was* halfway through the papers for that year. Maybe coming here hadn't been such a great idea, but quitting part way through the job I'd assigned myself wasn't going to prove a thing. I paid for my lunch and marched myself back to the second floor of the newspaper building.

Cherbourg was captured, and the Allied armies began to move forward in July. A skinny singer named Sinatra appeared at the Paramount Theater in New York, and it took forty-two policemen to control the mob of thirty thousand screaming "bobby soxers," whatever they were.

General George Patton's armored columns roared toward the Rhine. In Charleston, more bomber crews were graduated, but still nothing remotely referring to Roy Burnette appeared in the endless pages of print. There was a brief story on a training flight accident on August 17—a B-24 was reported missing on a cross-country flight from Charleston. What made me read it twice was the mention that the plane had been last reported at Blackwater Army Airfield where it had made a practice landing. The crew members' names were withheld for the moment, but the reporter had learned that the pilot's last name was "Barnes" or "Burns."

I leafed through another two days' worth.

Burns?

I turned the pages back and read the story again. The bomber had taken off from Charleston Army Air Base at midmorning. Five men were aboard. Three officers: the pilot, co-pilot, and navigator. And two enlisted men, the engineer and the radio operator. Standard training assignment, without the four gunners aboard. "Such training flights with partial crews are routine," the Charleston base public information officer had told the paper. "There is no need for the gunners to participate in all cross-country flights, particularly those with no aerial gunnery practice involved."

The second reading didn't tell me a heck of a lot more. I plowed into the next days, looking more carefully now. Then I hit pay dirt in the edition of August 20. The story was on page 1.

CRASH SURVIVOR AT KERNANVILLE

Kernanville, S.C., August 20. Lieutenant Raymond Burns, apparently the only survivor of a bomber training accident near here, stumbled into Kernanville late last night. Lt. Burns, pilot of the ill-fated flight, reported that his aircraft had caught fire about fifteen minutes after takeoff from Blackwater Army Airfield. He said he had landed the four-engined bomber at Blackwater as part of the training mission and was then flying on to Maxwell Field at Montgomery, Alabama. The aircraft has not yet been found.

Lt. Burns was not certain of the fate of the four others on board. He said it was his opinion that they had not survived. The incident is the third in a series of aircraft disappearances that have given rise to a superstition among flight crews that operations at the remote training field are affected by a "Blackwater Jinx."

The public relations officer at Charleston AFB, where the flight originated, stated early today that the search for the missing B-24 and its additional four crew members will continue.

A "Blackwater Jinx"? That was the same thing Aunt Agony Anthony had been talking about.

Through the week following Lt. Burns's appearance, there was a lot of guessing by the newspaper. Some interesting questions began to appear. Just where was the plane? How could the pilot be the only survivor when the pilot was supposed to be the last to leave an aircraft in trouble?

"This is becoming a third local mystery of the air," one reporter wrote. "No matter how carefully the Charleston public relations officer tries to explain it, the fact remains that no one knows what really happened near Kernanville on August 17. What makes the incident more baffling is the appearance of the survivor. There were no survivors of the two previous B-24 disappearances. Both were assumed to have gone down on over-water flights, sinking without a trace. Like Lt. Burns's ship, they too had taken off from Blackwater."

By early September, the missing B-24 still had not been found. An investigation board had convened, and Lt. Raymond Burns was the prime witness. There was a lack of detail, but I realized that it had been wartime, and military investigations probably hadn't been open to civilian reporters. What news came out of the investigation board meetings came out through the public relations officer. And he was something far short of a blabbermouth.

Lt. Burns claimed, it turned out, that he had been *blown* through a fuselage window by a sudden explosion aboard. He managed to get his parachute open, and he landed in a densely wooded area near Kernanville. He wandered until he stumbled upon an abandoned logging trail, which he followed into town. That much seemed true enough, though his claim about being catapulted through a window was debated for days. And his statement about a "blue-white flash" just before the explosion didn't make the story any more believable.

The officers on the investigation board finally decided the thing had been an accident, but the fact that the pilot had been the only survivor bothered them plenty. They recommended that Lt. Burns be taken off combat crew training. He was "assigned to new duties elsewhere," as the public relations officer said in mid-September.

I turned the musty page, and a photo leaped at me. The caption began, "Crew of ill-fated bomber, photographed at its last stop at Blackwater Army Airfield . . . "

The three officers and two enlisted men stood together beside the slab-sided nose of the bomber doomed to run into trouble that same day. Lieutenants Rowan, Pirelli, and Burns. Corporals Gilfus and Sheckler. Five of them, but I was interested in just one. I felt a chill even though I thought I was ready for the shock. Younger, thinner, a lot more hair, but there was no mistaking it. Lt. Raymond Burns was Roy Burnette.

"Did you find what you were looking for?" The librarian's voice startled me.

"Exactly," I told her. "Say, I wonder if you keep separate files on local stories?"

"Some of them. What is it that you're interested in?"

I pointed at the photo of Roy and his crew. She reached for the glasses, which dangled from her neck on a silver safety chain.

"Oh, I do remember that. I was about twenty-th—well, I was rather young at the time. I'm afraid that most of our files more than twenty-five years old are discarded. It's a shame. We don't have microfilm equipment yet, and we do have limited storage space. We only keep the pictures on file."

She took off her glasses and tapped her teeth with an earpiece. "You know, Mr. Reeves might be able to give you some detail on that story. I'll see if he's in the building."

Knighton J. Reeves was in the building, all right. His eagerness to see me should have been a warning. Trouble was, I'd never talked with a sharp reporter before.

I found him in the city room on the first floor, a paper-littered half-acre of desks and clacking typewriters with people ambling around in what looked like total confusion. That, I have since learned, is what every city room in every large newspaper is like.

"Mr. Reeves?"

He looked up from his typewriter, a gray owl with his ratty blue tie yanked down and his shirt collar open. A sour expression pulled his mouth toward his chin and put extra lines in his face. He ran spidery fingers through his thin foam of smog-colored hair and drew back a corner of his thin lips.

"Uh?"

"The woman in the library—"

"Ruthie Allen."

"I guess. Anyway, she said you might have some details on a story I'm interested in."

"Buy a paper, kid."

"This happened in 1944."

"Look in the library." He turned back to his typewriter and scowled at the yellow copy paper around its platen.

"I've looked in the library," I told him. "It's told me everything about Lieutenant Raymond Burns that it knows. The librarian—"

"Ruthie Allen."

"All right, Ruthie Allen. She thought you might have some more—"

His bored expression had changed. "Did you say Raymond Burns?" He swung toward me, and I noticed how sharp his eyes were—bright gleams of hard glass in that gray owl face. "What do you want to know about that creep for? You weren't even born then."

"I'm just interested."

"Writing a thesis on cowardice?"

"I'm not a writer. I'm a pilot."

"Oh? What kind?"

"Crop sprayer," I told him with maybe too much satisfaction. "Working out of Blackwater, defoliating cotton."

He smirked. "G'wan, kid. That's man's work. You can't be more'n what, maybe seventeen?"

"Nineteen. Look, either you can add something to that stuff up there in the library, or we're both wasting time." He was getting to me a little.

"Yeah," he said with a grin. "Yeah, I can add a detail or two if you really want it. But I'd like to know why you want it." Reeves's accent wasn't soft Carolina at all. It was hard New York. He'd been around. "You related to that Burns guy?"

"No relation. Just interested."

Reeves stared at me as if he were trying to make up his mind about something. Then his foot reached for the leg of a nearby chair and dragged it toward me. "Sit down. Tell you how this is going to work. I'll do you a favor. You do me one. O.K.?"

"If I can."

"Well, it was like this. If you really want the truth, that Burns thing was my first big story. I came down here from

55

a little Long Island paper. I was a 4F. You know what that meant? Unfit for military service. Heart murmur. Me with a heart murmur! Couldn't believe it. Anyway, here I was, bigger salary, but out of it—know what I mean? All the news was happening somewhere else. Europe, Africa, the Pacific. Even the U-boats did their Atlantic Coast torpedoing somewhere else. Then along came the Burns case."

He fumbled for a pencil and toyed with it while he talked.

"Yeah, along came Burns. I had a chance to get my teeth into something that had human interest and a nice touch of mystery, too."

"Mystery?"

"Sure. Still is. They never found Burns's plane, you know. He bailed out, and it flew on without him into nowhere. But it was different from the other two. You read that two other planes had disappeared before Burns's ship? Well, they went down at sea. At least, they were headed that way. So it's not too hard to imagine that they simply sank. No radio messages. Just zip! Gone. But this Burns thing was different. Here he came, wandering out of the woods with a wild story about being blown out of his own bomber. But it was never found, not a trace of it. Another victim of the 'Blackwater Jinx.' "

He looked at me sharply. "That made good copy, but my own opinion was—and is—phooey!"

"So what do you think happened to the plane?"

"It sure went down somewhere when the gas ran out, didn't it? And four guys, presumed dead, could have gotten out of the war and begun whole new lives for themselves if they landed in some remote spot, hid the plane, and then all kept their mouths shut."

"That's ridiculous," I said. "Burnette would have been in on a thing like that—otherwise it wouldn't have worked. He'd have had to bail out so they could—"

Reeves was grinning at me. "Maybe it is ridiculous, but so was the story he told."

"You don't believe he was blown out of the plane?"

"Personally, no. I figure he had to come up with some sort of explanation for ducking out of there. The explosion story was as good as any. But the fact remains that he was the only guy on that crew who ever showed up again. And he was the pilot. It just isn't done."

His eyes caught mine and held them, and he said, "Didn't you call him 'Burnette' a while back? You *know* this guy, don't you! Wait a minute, wait a minute. You said you're a crop sprayer in Blackwater. Ten to one that's where Ray Burns is, right?"

My stomach was doing a slow roll. "I didn't say anything like that."

"You didn't have to. Hmm. Might be a whale of a follow-up story here. 'Air Force Pilot Still Flies at Scene of Disgrace.' "

"You wouldn't write a thing like that!" But as I said it, I could see that Knighton J. Reeves would be only too happy to rake up all that past history for the sake of a new story. My mouth went dry.

"Want to thank you for the tip, kid. What did you say your name was?"

"I didn't."

"O.K., if you want to play that way, I'll just get it off the library register."

He had me there, and I felt childish. "Greg Stewart," I said as I stood up. I had the sick feeling that I was getting into something miles over my head, and I made a last plea. "Mr. Reeves, leave it alone, will you? What good can it do anybody?"

He pushed back his chair and got to his feet with a bounce. He came up to my Adam's apple, but that was plenty big enough to handle a typewriter. His voice was hard. "Pass up a story like this one can be? In a pig's eye, Stewart. In a pig's eye!"

5

THE CLOSER I GOT TO BLACKWATER, THE
more confused I found myself. Whoever said that revenge
is sweet may not have tried it. Learning about Roy's past
had made me more interested in him than in myself, but
blabbing to Knighton Reeves had probably done what I'd set
out to do.

Now that Reeves was on his trail, I had plenty of second
thoughts. I had dug up something on Roy, but just what did
I think I was going to do with it. Tell Al Derr? I suspected
that he'd known about Roy all along. Hadn't Al himself
told me that Roy had never quite recovered from a bad
break years ago?

Would I gain something by dragging Roy's past out on

view for Eddie Pelton and Carl Davis? They didn't have a grudge against him; I did. At least, I'd had it when I was driving the other way this morning. Then came the probing Mr. Reeves.

My hating Roy was one thing; sort of a family fight. When Reeves wanted to butt in, that was another thing. Who was he, anyway, to nose into our business!

Now that I had been far enough out of Blackwater to take a long look at things, I had to admit that I had come to South Carolina as a pretty cocky pilot. I'd been just plain careless when I'd knocked Roy flat that first day I swung the Pawnee around like a green kid. Could I really blame Roy for making sure I'd never be that careless again?

The drizzle had grown into a downpour when I pulled into Moultrie's dimly lit parking lot. I dashed into the restaurant side of the rickety building and squeezed water out of my shirt tail.

"Rainin'?" Moultrie raised his voice to be heard over the rattle of the storm on the tarpaper roof.

"Some," I said. "Hi, Eddie."

Eddie Pelton sat alone at the counter, and I joined him.

"Where you been all day?"

"Taking a look at Charleston," I told him, chancing a deep drag of Moultrie's chickory brew. "Anybody else around?"

"Carl went over to Columbia, I think. Knows some family over there. Rest of 'em are at the base, waiting for the weather to break. Won't though, until late tomorrow."

"Roy out there, too?" I had made a tough decision, and I was going to see it through.

"Yep. He's helping Frank and Harry put your ship back together. Didn't know Roy had a mechanic's license, did you?"

"Lot of things about Roy I don't know," I said. "Guess I'd better get myself out there, too." I slapped down the coffee money and went back into the rain.

The drive to the base was black and soggy. Jouncing past the ruins of the old squadron area gave me the same skittering chill I'd felt that first night. I found Roy in the hangar rebuilding the outer left wing panel with Frank Kingston handing him tools like a bean pole of a male nurse. Harry Feather's crew-cut torpedo-shaped head peered from behind the engine. "I know Roy's a miracle man with a wrench, Frankie Boy, but you got more to do than *watch* miracles tonight. Let's see you do a couple of your own on this engine."

Frank shuffled over to the nose of the stripped Pawnee, and I cleared my throat. "Roy . . . " My voice dried out, and I had to begin again. This was worse than the time I'd had to tell my dad I had run the power mower into the duck pond. "Roy, I've got to talk to you."

He looked up, his long face hard in the glare of the bare bulbs hanging on the two workstands.

"Can't it wait?"

"Afraid not. Something's happened you ought to know about."

"Like what?"

I glanced at Frank and Harry. "In private."

"Go ahead, Roy," Harry said. "Frank and I can handle the rest of it."

His mouth gave a little twitch of irritation, but he laid his socket wrench on the workstand and wiped his hands on a rag he pulled from a pocket of his coveralls.

"This had better be something worthwhile. We got a couple hours yet to put in on that Pawnee you bent up. Come on, we'll use Al's office. He's left."

I walked across the small office and leaned against the far wall with my hands in my pockets. Roy put a bony shoulder against the door jamb and opened a bag of salted peanuts.

"Well?" He stared at me and began to chomp. My palms were wet, and I could barely keep my voice under control.

"I went into Charleston today."

"So?"

"To the offices of the *Southeastern Advocate*. To the library of that newspaper."

"You went to a newspaper office. What about it?" His expression didn't change, but there was something just a little different about his voice.

"I went through the files for 1944."

"And?" He threw out the one word like the bark of an irritated police dog, but I could see that something in him had just crumpled.

"And I found what I thought I was looking for."

His hand stopped halfway to his mouth. "What's that mean?" Most of the old Roy was still here, but the voice was new. The edge had gone.

I said, "I think it means . . . it means that I wanted to get something on you, Roy."

In the silence that followed, I faked a cough and scratched my nose. But I couldn't get my eyes off the floor.

I knew he was studying my face. "Somehow you picked up a few rumors about me, right? Then you heard me spout off yesterday to Dobbs about 1944. You put it all together and found Ray Burns in that newspaper library. That's pretty slick work." He rattled the peanut bag, then crumpled it in his hand. "Pretty frightening, too. What kind of kid are you?"

I looked up. "I don't know, Roy. But when I got what I was looking for, I found that I didn't want it."

"No stupid idea of blackmail?"

A cold shudder caught my shoulder blades. "My gosh, Roy! I'm not a . . . a blackmailer." I almost whispered the word.

"What, then? Why did you dig it all up?"

"A half-baked idea of getting even with you, somehow. It was a kid's trick, Roy. I think I've grown up a lot in a day."

"Yeah, maybe." He slumped into the chair behind Al's desk and gazed at the opposite wall. "I've been riding you hard. Too hard, I guess. But I could see a lot of myself in you. That dumb way you came in here that first night. That was me thirty years ago." His face sagged. He looked old and worn out. "When you flipped that Pawnee around and knocked me flat, well, that was me, too, when I was a green cadet."

He stood up and paced across the little administration shack. "I've just wanted you to be the best darn pilot I could beat you into being." He turned to face me. "You understand any of this?"

"I'm beginning to."

"Well, that can end it, then. You are turning into a good pilot. In spite of yourself. Maybe I can begin to be more of a partner instead of a teacher. Look, you forget about Ray Burns and I'll forget that you pushed into something that's better left alone." He reached for the screen door.

"Wait, Roy. That can't end it. I wish it could, but it can't. I ran into a guy at the paper in Charleston. Named Reeves."

Roy let the door slap shut. "Knighton Reeves? He couldn't still work there! Not after all these years."

63

"He does."

"And he's just as sharp as he used to be, isn't he? I can tell that by looking at you, kid. He knows I'm down here."

I nodded. "Before I realized what he was up to, I laid it right in his lap. When I left there, he was getting bright ideas about a big follow-up story."

"Uh." Roy plopped back into Al's chair. "That does it. If Reeves is only half the reporter he used to be, I'll be spread all over the papers again."

He seemed to kind of fade out. Then as I stood there twitching, trying to figure out something useful to say, he came back to life.

"You want to hear what happened back in 1944? The papers had it more or less right, but they drew a conclusion that didn't help me any. Not at all."

The soft rain pattered on the roof of the shack. The desk lamp threw shadows across the room as Roy's words, strangely hushed, took us back three decades.

"We took off from Charleston just before noon. Five of us—Art Rowan, the co-pilot; Joe Pirelli, our navigator. The radio operator's name was Gilfus. We called him 'Fussy.' And there was Bob Sheckler, the flight engineer. I was the pilot. Had just a couple hundred flying hours. Pretty green, all of us.

"We landed here about half an hour later. Hard to believe now." He turned to the window and stared into the night. "Right out there—thirty years ago. We had lunch in the officers' mess up in the squadron area—up there where those ruins are now. Then we came back here, posed out by the plane for some local photographer, and took off for Bermuda."

"Bermuda? The newspaper stories said you were going on to Alabama."

"We took off for Bermuda, but about five minutes out, we got word by radio that the island was socked in by unexpected weather. Our flight plan was switched inland to Montgomery, Alabama. So we swung around and headed west."

He stood up, then sat on a corner of the desk, one leg dangling, and fiddled with a stapling machine. "The weather had turned murky, a mixture of heavy haze and smoke from the paper mills along the coast. East wind that day. That always gunked up the sky for us. The farther west we flew, the worse it got.

"The flight was routine until we were maybe fifteen minutes out. Art Rowan and Joe Pirelli were joking on the intercom about the Blackwater Jinx. Then Sheckler broke in. 'I smell gas back here,' he said. 'Lots of it.'

"That scared all of us. Those old B-24's were famous for going off like cherry bombs because of sudden gas leaks. I think I panicked a little myself. I turned the controls over to Rowan and ducked back into the bomb bay. In the B-24, the bomb bay was like the inside of a box car with a catwalk down the middle between the bomb racks. I found raw gas all over the bottom of the bay, maybe a quarter of an inch deep. The stuff was pouring out of a broken fuel line somewhere over my head, a steady stream of it."

Roy slapped his palm on Al's stapling machine. "We had to get those bomb bay doors open to air out that plane in a hurry. The quickest way to do it was to call Art Rowan on the intercom. The nearest intercom plug-in was aft, in the waist of the plane. I got back there in one heck of a hurry, plugged my mike into the box at the right waist window, and—that's when she blew. First, I remember a kind of bluish flash, then the whole bomb bay went. The blast must have punched the plastic window panel right out of its frame—and me out right behind it. I found myself five thousand feet over South Carolina with the roar of my own plane fading above me.

"I grabbed for the D-ring, fell forever, and then the chute finally popped. I was swinging down through the murk. I remember thinking that it was a good thing *I'd* been blown into thin air instead of one of the enlisted crew members."

"Why?" My throat was dry, and my voice cracked.

"Because they wore just chute harnesses in the plane. Their chutes were separate chest packs. You had to hook a chest pack onto the harness before you jumped. Pilots wore a back pack. The chute was built in. If one of the others had been blown out the way I was, he'd never have had a chance to grab his chest chute on the way. It didn't make any difference, though, in a few minutes. Before I came down in the woods, I heard a kind of dull boom way off in the distance. I knew my B-24 had crashed."

"Didn't you tell the Air Force all this?"

"Of course I did. You're not hearing anything that isn't a matter of official record, even if the papers didn't think much of it."

"Then why—"

"My word was all anybody had to go on, and you can see that it was a pretty wild story. The Air Force didn't know what to think because the plane was never found."

"But you heard it go down."

"Nobody *saw* it. The day was too hazy. And we were over a wild part of the state. Almost like a jungle. There are records of other planes that have gone down in the U.S. and were never found. One of them is still somewhere in Okefenokee Swamp, on the Florida-Georgia border. They searched for my ship for more than two weeks. Not a trace.

66

It became an even more interesting part of the Blackwater Jinx legend."

"And along came Reeves," I said.

"You aren't kidding. He hounded and pounded, and what should have been a simple investigation hearing turned into a big case of—well, suspected cowardice. So the Air Force was pushed into doing what they did. Exiled me into the Service Command. No combat for a guy who might have deserted his crew."

Roy leaned against the door jamb again and looked into the rain. "I know that plane's still out there," he said almost to himself. "I'm *sure* of it. And I'm going to find it. I got this job so I can spend my off time looking for it."

"How long have you been looking?"

He turned, and his eyes held an odd glitter. "All last summer and most of this one."

"You waited thirty years before you tried this?"

"I've been all over the world trying to get it out of my system. Africa, Pakistan, India, anywhere I could get a flying job. But a guy in Africa made me realize I can't ever forget it. I tried to get work flying food into Biafra with a mercenary outfit just outside Nigeria. The recruiter remembered me, actually remembered me after all those years. 'No job for you, Burns,' he said. 'We're hiring hawks, not chickens.' So I can't ever wipe it out—unless I find that plane."

He had gripped the back of a chair so hard that his knuckles were bone white. His jaw muscles pulsed. I'd never seen Roy like this, and it shook me. His whole life was focused on that old B-24, and maybe it wasn't even out there. After all, the only thing he had to go on was a thud he had thought he heard in the distance after being blown through a window. It could have been a lot of things. A farmer blasting stumps. An old tree falling in the woods below him. Even his own ears popping with the altitude change.

Or . . . I tried not to think it, but the suspicion came anyway. The Air Force had tried to be neutral about believing Roy's story, but an experienced reporter hadn't had any trouble making up his mind. Now I was in the act. Roy was looking at me for a decision of my own. "You've heard my side of it now. What do you think?"

I hedged. "Do you really care what I think?"

"Well, I'll tell you something, Greg," he said slowly. "You're the first guy who hasn't jumped to a conclusion on the thing. Yes, I do care what you think."

"I think," I said, "that I'd like to help you look for that lousy airplane." As I said it, I knew Roy could sense that I was still turning the whole story over in my mind. It was entirely possible that he was chasing a hopeless old burned-out dream of clearing his name; that he was—well, obsessed with this crazy idea that out there in the swamp lay the answer to all his problems.

Another thought hit me. Maybe Reeves was right. Maybe something sinister had happened that day that Roy couldn't face.

But now Roy said, "You'd better think hard about getting involved in this. Ray Burns was a real black sheep in those days—the guy who abandoned his crew. That was the worst act of cowardice a pilot could pull. I didn't have a friend anywhere. My reputation moved faster than I could. The Air Force did me a favor by assigning me to a supply base in the Aleutian Islands, but even there it was no picnic. It's been easier since I changed my name and went into civilian flying. But there are still a lot of guys around who remember Lt. Raymond Burns."

"Who else here knows who you really are . . . were?" I asked.

"Just Al Derr—and you. But now that Reeves is on my trail, I guess it'll all blow up again."

"I'm sorry," I said. It sounded so feeble, but I really meant it.

"Inevitable. I've known that all along." He hunched his shoulders and jammed his hands in his jacket pockets. "O.K., kid," he said, as if he'd come to a decision. "If you insist on being a part of this, I've got something to show you. It came in yesterday, and I have the feeling it's going to make the search a lot less hopeless."

6

WE STOOD IN ROY'S CABIN, LOOKING INTO the wooden crate he had just opened for me. The thing lying in the straw packing appeared to be a yard-long bomb with a single tail fin at the tapered end.

"That's to keep it from twisting at the end of the cable," Roy said. "Let's see. Here's the amplifier box, the reel, and . . . " He rummaged through the packing material and pulled out a cardboard carton. "And two hundred feet of suspension cable and receiver wire, and the headset."

He stood up and surprised me with a quick grin. I'd never seen Roy really smile before.

"It looks great," I said. "But what is it?"

"MAD gear. Magnetic Airborne Detector. The Navy

developed the idea for submarine defense. Installed it on blimps and patrol planes during World War II and for a few years afterward. It detects large metallic objects. I knew that the surplus original military equipment was much too bulky to operate in a small civil plane, but last winter I read where an engineer near Philadelphia had developed a miniature version for aerial survey of iron ore veins. I wanted to try it down here, and he agreed to let me work with this experimental rig."

"And now you're going to try this over the place you think your B-24 went down."

"We both are. I've been searching that area with binoculars for two summers—every free hour I could get. Al lets me borrow the Super Cub. I pay for gas and oil. Here take a look at this."

He spread a map across the small table in the corner of the room. "It's a county plat map of the Great Silver Swamp northwest of Kernanville. That's where the B-24 has *got* to be."

The map showed a desolation of watery lowlands, dense woods and brush. Isolated ponds and sloughs were scattered through it. The logging settlement of Kernanville lay to the east, and Derby was twenty miles north. No roads were charted through the swamp, and there weren't any major waterways, either. Just a deserted tangle ten miles across and six miles north to south, with a few streams wandering through it.

"It's sixty square miles of swamp, Roy. That's a heck of a lot of territory."

"I know how big it is. I've spent maybe fifty hours over it."

"And you haven't seen anything but swamp."

His voice took on an edge. "Now it's going to be dif-

71

ferent. We have the MAD. It gives me a whole fresh start."
He grabbed a pencil and drew a grid on the map. "Look,
we'll divide the Great Silver into sections. Two-mile-square
blocks, like this." He outlined the swamp and then made
two horizontal and four vertical lines, cutting the map into
fifteen squares. "The MAD sweeps a strip two hundred feet
wide when it's flown a hundred feet off the ground. At least,
that's what the guy in Pennsylvania says. So with two-
hundred-foot-wide sweeps, we can cover one of these two-
mile grid squares in fifty-three passes. When you break it
down that way, it doesn't seem so impossible."

I watched his lean face in the white glare of the ceiling
bulb. Rain filtered through the tall oaks that arched over
Aunt Agony's cabins. A chilly wind shook big drops loose
and they plopped on the roof. There was a sharpness in
Roy's eyes. Was it just eagerness to try out the new equipment that lay on the floor in its open case? Or were those
deep-set eyes burning themselves out in a search that had
no end? Could Roy be hunting on and on for something
that didn't exist?

The wind blew the weather eastward and out to sea. By
afternoon of the next day, we were back over the cotton
fields. The breeze faded around four, and muggy heat rose
out of the lowlands. I shared a spread west of Blackwater
with Carl Davis. The sun was halfway down in the dull
western sky when we began our passes. When we finished
the assignment, it rested fat and orange on the horizon.

We flew back to the base and tied down our Pawnees. I
followed Carl toward the office shack, but stopped before
I got there. A short, skinny guy had come out of the
shadows of the hangar, and he walked toward me as if he'd
been waiting a long time to do it. "Go on ahead," I told

72

Carl. "Tell Al I'll be there in a minute to do my part of the paperwork."

The little guy was big enough to sour the evening for me. He was Knighton Reeves, out here from Charleston, and certainly not up to anything good.

"We meet again, Stewart," he said in that grating voice of his. "You have any idea where Ray Burns is?"

I had mentally kicked myself a dozen times for tangling with Reeves in Charleston. Now I did it again. But it didn't do a bit of good. Reeves just got more insistent.

"I asked you where Ray Burns is, Stewart."

He had a way of getting me mad in a hurry. "How would I know where the heck he is!" I yipped at him. "I'm not the keeper of the roster around here. Ask in the office."

"I did ask in the office and the old guy in there—Derr, I think his name is—told me he never heard of Ray Burns. He didn't fool me any more than you do."

At this point, Al Derr stuck his head out of the office shack and called me. "Hey," he said after I got inside, "who is that character? He came barging in here like a bull—well, a small bull. Said he was a reporter and asked for you. What goes on?"

I looked quickly at Carl, standing at the far end of the counter, and Al cleared his throat. "That's all for tonight, Carl. You can shove off. We'll finish your billing records in the morning."

When Carl has headed for the parking area, Al said to me, "From what that reporter asked, I gather that somehow you've stumbled onto Roy's background—the part of it that he's spent thirty years keeping quiet. He hasn't used the name 'Ray Burns' since World War II. Now that you got this little bomb, what do you expect to do with it?"

"I'm afraid I've done too much already," I admitted, and I told him about my trip to Charleston and the dumb business there with Knighton Reeves. "So I blew it and I'm sorry," I finished. "I mean, I'm really sorry. I've stirred up this whole rat's nest because of a kid's idea of getting even. Now I don't like how it feels."

Al looked at me with a face that seemed to have collapsed. "Have you any idea—*any* idea—what this can do to Roy? He's spent three decades burying the name of Ray Burns. In just one day you've brought that nightmare back to him."

"I don't think he's ever been free of it, Al. Still, I'm not proud of what I've done. I told him that."

"Well, that's something. What did he say?"

"He said I could help him look for the B-24."

Al walked over to the door and stared across the old runway. "Yeah, the B-24. That lousy B-24. He can't get that out of his mind. The idea of its being out there somewhere haunts him. I wish he'd give up that idea. Let the past alone. Begin to enjoy life a little. What does it matter what happened so many years ago?"

"It matters to Roy," I said. "And you know something, Al? It's beginning to matter to me."

Al sighed and shoved his hands deep into his pockets. The leathery old face folded into a frown. "Heck, it matters to me, too, kid. I've been lending him the Super Cub to make his crazy search with."

I watched him. "You don't think that bomber's out there, do you?"

"I don't know what I think. I just know that lending Roy the Super Cub is a good way to let him blow off some steam now and then."

I went back outside, and Reeves trotted up as soon as

74

he saw me. "What were you hatching in there? A plot to keep me from interviewing Ray Burns?"

"If you'd stop being so suspicious and look around," I told him, "you'd see Roy's Pawnee coming in now."

The incoming sprayer's wings glinted in the last gleam of the setting sun. The plane leveled off and sank to the runway.

When Roy cut the switch at the tie-down line, I walked up to him fast. "Sorry, Roy, but that reporter I told you about is here waiting for you. There's no way to get out of it."

Roy pulled off his crash helmet and dropped it back in the cockpit. "It's been a long time coming, but I guess I've known all along I couldn't try to straighten out the past and keep the effort completely private."

He stepped off the wing and went straight to Reeves. "I'm Roy Burnette. You want to talk to me?"

The gray-haired reporter squinted up through his glasses. After long silent seconds, he nodded. "Ray Burns. Thirty years erased, just like that. Well, Burns, they say the criminal always returns to the scene, don't they?"

That crack got to me, not Roy. "Wait a minute!" I yelled. "That's a heck of a thing—"

"Calm down, Greg," Roy said. "You're just beginning to hear the kind of thing I went through. You'll have to get used to it if Reeves insists on stirring it all up again."

"I'm not doing the stirring," Reeves said. "You're the guy who came back here and brought the whole business back to life. I only report stories; I don't take part in them."

Roy's jawline took that hard set I'd seen so many times. "You're taking part in this one, Reeves. When I find that B-24, you're going to have to eat every word you ever wrote about me. And I *am* going to find it."

Reeves smirked and turned to me. "One thing you got to say for him is that he doesn't give up easy."

"That isn't what you were writing about him in 1944," I reminded him. "Or do you just write stories the way you think they'll sell the most papers?"

"I write them as I see them," Reeves shot back. "I don't know how I see this one yet. You want to help fill me in, or am I going to have to work on my own?"

Roy took a long look at him. "What I'm doing is simple enough," he finally said. "Logic tells me that bomber crashed west of Kernanville. That's where I'm looking for it."

Reeves asked in his best reporter-taking-notes style, "Why now?"

"I've been searching down here for a couple of seasons."

"Oh? What prompted your sudden crusade? If you think that bomber has been out there three decades, why weren't you down here a long time ago trying to clear your name?"

"A lot of things," Roy said. "Time, money. And I've been out of the country quite a few years. Bush flying in Canada, a small airline in Pakistan, flying for a mining out-fit in South America. I just haven't been available."

"You aren't convincing me, Burns," said Reeves. "There's another bigger reason, isn't there?"

"Like what?"

"Like let me guess. You thought that chapter in your life was a closed book. Then somewhere you ran into a guy who remembered, and it shook you—shook you good. You realized that a lot of guys still remembered and hated you. Aha! I can tell by your face that I'm hitting home. If you don't find that mythical bomber of yours, the past will keep coming back, won't it? Every time you meet a guy who remembers. And every time you meet some old pilot, you have to ask yourself: 'Is he going to be one of them?' That's it, isn't it, Burns?"

Roy pressed his lips together hard. "It would take a guy like you to turn a quiet, private search into a big deal all over again, wouldn't it?"

"Aah, any good reporter would jump on a story like this one. You know that. Besides, you got yourself out on this skinny limb. Who asked you to go through this nutty search, anyway? It's all your own wild goose chase. I only report the facts."

"That," Roy said, "will be a welcome change."

I took a good look at Reeves's face, and something hit me right between the ears. I realized that, as of this minute, I was one hundred percent on Roy's side. As far as I was concerned, that old bomber existed. It was somewhere out there in those swamps, and we were going to find it and make this cocky, smirking reporter choke on every word he'd written.

The next day, I worked with Carl Davis, then flew with Eddie Pelton for two more. On Thursday, I wobbled back to my cabin, bleary eyed, itching from the darned defoliant that had crystallized on my flying clothes. I'd forced down a quick cheese sandwich at Moultrie's, and I had been almost too tired to chew it. I flopped face down on the creaky bed with all my clothes on and wondered whether I should sleep that way or take a shower and get into pajamas.

Before I could make up my mind, a knock at the door woke me up, and I felt groggier than before. It was Roy. "Tomorrow," he said. "We both have a day off coming. We'll duck out of here at 6:00 A.M. and see how good that MAD gear really is."

7

ROY AND I GOT TO MOULTRIE'S AT THE SAME time the truck from Charleston raced past and bounced Moultrie's package of *Southeastern Advocate* early morning editions into his parking lot. I took the package into the restaurant with us. Moultrie snapped the wire binding with an old pair of cutting pliers he kept under the counter. He began leafing through a copy as Roy and I drank our coffee.

Moultrie was studying us. He puffed once out each side of his mouth. "Oh, brother!" he said, which I'd never heard him say before. "Looks like Roy's got hisself a handful of problems." He shoved the paper across the counter for us to see.

Reeves's story was on page one. He had done a real job. PILOT SEARCHES FOR GHOST PLANE, read the headline. The story was complete with Reeves-type comments such as, "Not content with leaving his shaky personal history alone . . . " and "Burnette-Burns has been irresistibly drawn back to the scene of his own disaster."

During the last few days, Reeves had done more nosing around. "This reporter has learned," he wrote, "that a bulky package arrived for Burnette in Blackwater by rail express some days ago. Though confirmation was not available, it is thought that the shipment consisted of search apparatus to aid in the hunt for the alleged lost bomber."

"That's a neat piece of one-sided writing," Roy said to me. "If he'd called me, I would have told him all about the MAD. What's the difference, now that he knows the rest of it?"

"Maybe he figured that it reads better this way. Keeps the story more mysterious. What I don't like is that business about the 'alleged' bomber."

"He's got to say that. Otherwise, he'd be almost admitting that it exists."

Moultrie had listened to all this, now and then quietly blowing through the corner of his mouth. "So you're Ray Burns," he finally said. "Heard about you, 'course. Before my time here, though. Well, well, well."

We finished our coffee and got back in Roy's car. "I wonder what that 'Well, well, well' was supposed to mean?" I said.

"I don't know, but I figure Moultrie is happy to get a buck, no matter whom it comes from. Whatever the rest of them think around here, I'll just have to live with it."

The sun was beginning to burn off the early morning ground fog out at the base. I helped Roy lug the crate of

MAD equipment to the Super Cub. While I took out the rear cockpit control stick and stored it in the luggage hamper, Roy tapped out the hinge pins of the upper and lower door sections. He gave me the key to the hangar, and I stowed the doors in a corner. When I came back, Roy had clamped the cable reel to the bottom of the door opening. We set the amplifier unit on the floor, just inside the lip of the big hole where the doors had been, and checked the battery. A powerful spark jumped from the end of the blade of the screwdriver Roy touched across the contacts.

"Get in there, Greg, and see if you're going to able to ride with this monster."

When we rested it on its blunt nose, the sensor "bomb" fit between my knees with its single-finned tail in my face. I hung the headset around my neck, fastened the safety belt, and checked the knee pocket of my coveralls to make sure I had the duplicate map on which Roy had ruled the search grid for me. Everything was shipshape, and I tapped Roy's shoulder.

"Ready if you are."

The engine kicked, then caught. We taxied out on the runway, swung around to face the light breeze. Just before Roy shoved the throttle forward, he hunched around and gave me a quick sort of half smile. It said a lot.

Then the tail lifted. Hard wind began to blast through the door opening. I watched the rushing river of blacktop fall away beneath the right wheel. Roy stuck the nose high, and the trees beyond the end of the runway shrank to a toy forest.

The greens and browns of the South Carolina lowlands unrolled below us. Here and there, a pond or creek flashed a quick reflection of the sun. I saw a little herd of deer in an open field bolt for the woods as we buzzed overhead. Our shadow chased us to Kernanville and hopscotched across the roofs of the buildings along the main street. North of town began the scattered bush where Roy had wandered until he stumbled into Kernanville so many years ago.

Ten miles farther on, out of the wetlands rose a green-black wall of cypress, pine, and oaks, with a towering dead trunk here and there blasted stark white by years of sun and wind. From these twisted arms, Spanish moss drooped like torn flags. Roy edged to the left, and we flew along the south side of the Great Silver Swamp. I looked into the overgrown wasteland, and I shuddered. Just the idea of going in there on foot was enough to give you a bad case of the crawls.

A few minutes later, we swung northwest around the far edge of the swamp, and Roy turned his head to shout above the engine's howl and the rush of air through the doorway. "Reel out the MAD."

I eased the bomb-shaped sensor over the side and slipped the little clutch on the cable reel. The sensor pod grew tiny below us. When the two-hundred-foot cable was all paid out, I put on the headset and flipped the amplifier switch. I heard a low hum and a little crackle of static. I pulled the map out of my knee pocket and fixed it to my thigh with a couple of fat rubber bands I'd brought along.

We started in the upper-left northwest square of the grid Roy had drawn on my map. The mile-long passes three hundred feet above the trees were a novelty at first. We made the first one along the northern edge of the swamp where abandoned cotton fields dwindled into a thin strip of overgrown old pastureland. Two weather-blackened wooden sheds had crumbled at the fringe of the open area; then the ancient pasture melted into the marshy beginning of the Great Silver Swamp.

Each pass, two hundred feet south of the previous sweep, took us deeper over the wasteland. A fire had gutted this area years before, leaving bare tree trunks jutting stiffly above the thick vines. Here and there, a hidden stream or a sudden small pond reflected quick flashes of sunlight.

After two and a half hours, when I didn't think my ears would take more than another minute of it, Roy leaned back and shouted over the engine racket. "Reel the thing in. We'll put down at Derby for fuel and lunch."

We were back over the Great Silver Swamp an hour later with a full tank of gas. After three more hours, I began to see all sorts of interesting spots dancing along the skyline. When I eased the headset pressure, my ears ached as if they'd been frozen. We hadn't gotten a single yip out of the MAD. Well, except on a test run over a cotton-picking machine north of the swamp, where I'd picked up a squeal that nearly blew me out of the cockpit.

But now the sun was dropping into the clouds along the horizon, and we were beat. I wound in the sensor, and Roy pointed the Super Cub toward Blackwater. We landed in the coppery gloom that always moved out of the woods and lay over the runway at sunset. As we taxied to the tie-down ramp in front of the administration shack, I noticed that Frank Kingston and Harry Feather had come out of the maintenance hangar and were staring at the parking area. I stuck my head through the doorway and looked around the Cub's high nose.

A whole gang of people were leaving a lot more cars than were usually parked behind the ramp. We swung into position over a set of tie-down ropes. Roy cut the switch and climbed out, peering under the wing at the dozen guys bearing down on us.

"Now what the heck do they want?" he muttered. I handed him the bomb-shape sensor and jumped at the flash. The thing hadn't exploded—our picture had been taken. Then another photographer fired his electronic wonder . . . and still another. Oh, Reeves had done his work well. The wire services were interested now, and they all were here: Associated Press, United Press International, and some southern group. Another guy kept insisting that Roy go right to Columbia for a TV interview. It was a nutty few minutes with everybody yelling at the same time and shoving tape recorder mikes in our faces. Two characters stood off a few feet and held movie cameras with blinding floodlights at the ready position against their cheeks.

Roy tried walking past them to the shack, but they blocked him. I could see an explosion climbing bright red up the back of his neck. Then he blew.

"Shut up, all of you!"

And they did.

"Now," Roy said quietly in the sudden silence, "I'll make a statement if you'll give me a chance." The microphones came up again, three of them, like metal cobras. I heard the two movie cameras start to whir. "I see that all of you read the Reeves story in the *Southeastern Advocate* this morning." Roy went on. "I hate to disillusion you, but there's really no mystery to what I'm doing. This thing is just a recent modification of the Navy's old Magnetic Airborne Detection system. I'm using it to search the area where my B-24 went down."

One of the TV reporters said, "You have any evidence at all that plane is out there?"

"A good memory," Roy answered.

"According to what I've read," the TV guy persisted, "all there is to remember was a dull boom in the haze. That's according to your own testimony, though. Have you anything more substantial than that to go on?"

Roy looked right into the cameras. "I know it's out there."

When they finally packed up their tapes, film, and notebooks, they had Roy on record three ways. Al Derr stuck his head out of the office as we carried the MAD toward Roy's car.

"They aren't gonna let up on you until you find that derned bomber, are they, Roy? I tried to head 'em off when they called earlier, but they came on in anyway." He eyed the equipment we carried. "That gear help any?"

"It will," Roy said grimly. We set the stuff down on the macadam, and Roy studied the assignment board posted by the door of the shack. "I see the season's petering out. No assignments Saturday. I'll take the Cub again."

Amazing how fast those news people worked. Next morning, Aunt Agony told me the story had been on the eleven o'clock TV news, and of course the morning paper from Charleston carried the wire service story, along with a column of sidelights Reeves had worked up from his own files. The front page picture was just fine. Roy was cradling the MAD sensor in his arms as though it was some kind of baby he was protecting, and I was craning my head out of the Super Cub as though I couldn't stand being left out of the picture.

They began to drift into town that evening: spongers ready to sop up a few bucks on the story somebody else had uncovered, the feature guys looking for "in-depth" stuff, and the just plain curious. First to appear was a writer-photographer team from a Chicago magazine, two very pale guys, both overweight and soft, wearing expensive sports shirts with jazzy-looking kerchiefs at the neck. They took a cabin behind mine for a night or two.

A nervous little guy, who told Moultrie he was a free-lance writer on a retainer from a West Coast aviation magazine, got the cabin farthest from the house. Aunt Agony was raking it in. Blackwater had become a boom-let town overnight. A day later, a few more characters had hit town, asked their questions, and poked about. They didn't stay in Blackwater, but worked out of motel rooms near Charleston. I guessed they were doing what I had done to stir up this rat's nest in the first place: searching old newspaper files.

All in all, the second wave of story seekers brought in quite an assortment of typewriter jockeys and film burners. They kept showing up at unexpected times at the base and in Blackwater. Roy and I had names for some of them. The Chicago pair were "Stuff" and "Nonsense." The skinny free-lancer from the West Coast was "Scoop." One of the guys who commuted from Charleston was a wire service man built like a wrestler. We called him "The Grizzly." Another character, a photographer, wore khakis as we did, and a heavy beard as we did not. Naturally, we called him "The Beard." Scoop, The Grizzly, and The Beard hung around together. The first time they showed up, Scoop and The Grizzly spent the better part of an hour arguing with The Beard because he wouldn't go near Aunt Agony's cabins. "When I'm on the expense account," he growled, "I don't stay in no third-rate cabins run by no crazy old woman. I'm staying in a motel in Charleston. You can go first class with me or sleep on the rocks in one of them shacks."

He sold them on the Charleston motel, and working from

there, they commuted to Blackwater, choked on Moultrie's chickory blend—I finally had discovered you really had to build up an immunity to it—and generally made huge nuisances of themselves.

The Grizzly took dozens of pages of notes. The Beard took roll after roll of photos with his fancy Hasselblad. Stuff and Nonsense couldn't stop talking into the little mini-tape recorders they wore in hip holsters.

After three or four days, we got used to them the way you get used to pebbles in your shoe. But we couldn't dump these pebbles out, so we learned to live with them around.

Roy had a couple of assignments Thursday. I flew two spray jobs Friday. The season really was dying, and it wouldn't be long before everybody packed up and left Blackwater until next year. Al, his two mechanics, and Dobbs Musserman would go back to home base in Illinois, of course. Eddie Pelton had a deal with some outfit in Alaska to fly supplies to mining engineers in some outpost up there. Carl Davis was going to take it easy on the West Coast. I didn't know yet what I'd do. And Roy? He wasn't thinking any further than the Great Silver Swamp and Saturday.

And on Saturday, he tapped on my cabin door at a chilly four in the A.M. We loaded the MAD into his car and eased out of Aunt Agony's grass-stubbled parking area in the pitch blackness. Kernanville passed five hundred feet below the Super Cub just as the first thin strip of dawn edged the horizon behind us.

8

WE WERE OVER THE FIFTH QUADRANT ON our maps by eleven o'clock. And we had found nothing. The buzz-crackle went on and on, clamped into the middle of my head by the earphones. The Great Silver Swamp unrolled beneath us endlessly, its twisted trees jutting up like bony fingers. The little blue MAD sensor raced along just above their tops, its electronic signals searching deep into rotting spider lilies, swamp azaleas, and miles of thick vines. But it found nothing.

Then we raced over a canopy of wild grape vines, and the MAD let out a squeal that sent a solid shock right through the roots of my hair! That was it—one yelp, then back to snap, crackle, pop, and buzz.

I pounded Roy's back. "Hey! I heard it! I heard it!"

He turned, and at that dumb instant the engine decided to act up. It blurped and choked, and Roy grabbed for the carburetor heat knob. "Ice in the carburetor intake," he yelled. "From the moisture in the air over the swamp." I thought back to my flight student days. Yep, you can get carb ice even on a warm summer day because the air goes so fast through the intake that its temperature can get down to freezing.

The engine quit hacking and ran smoothly again. Roy whirled in his seat. "Where was it?" I hesitated a bare second. "Come on, Greg, come on! Where did you hear it?"

I looked over the side. How do you find a particular leaf in a whole bowl of spinach. "Half a mile behind us."

"I'm going back two sweeps before you heard that signal," Roy shouted back. "If you hear it again, hit me once and mark your map."

We flew back to the corner of the search quadrant that Roy remembered had been marked by a group of three tall cypresses. He headed south, then east to repeat the pass we had made a few minutes before I had heard the squeal from the MAD.

A couple minutes later, the thing screamed in my ears again. I looked frantically for some kind of landmark, pounded Roy's shoulder, and tried to mark my map with a pencil stub, all at the same time.

We circled, and I spotted a tall skinny tree with a buzzard's nest near its top. On the map, the place I had marked was about two miles into the swamp from the north, but only a mile in from the west.

"Nowhere to land around here," Roy shouted. "We'll have to go to Derby and get a truck."

We set down at the Derby Airport a few minutes later

and found that Art Ford, the manager, had a jeep that he would rent to us. He was a paunchy businessman type who wore an old-fashioned white shirt and tie to work, and he was the last guy in South Carolina we would have expected to own a jeep for bird photography.

"You're kidding!" Roy said.

"Huh uh. I go out early in the morning before I open this place for business. Take a Nikon with a 250-millimeter lens."

I said to Roy, "We'd better get some snake boots and heavier clothes."

"Getting late."

Ford said, "Better make time, boys. It's loaded in there with cottonmouths. Maybe rattlers, too."

"I always have time for snakeboots," I said with a shudder.

We bought two pairs of the heavy knee-high boots at the grubby Crimmins Hardware Store in Derby a mile from the airport. Roy paid another buck for a surplus Army compass. We tossed the big paper bag in the back of the jeep and bounced south.

A little before three o'clock, we turned off the county road that ran near the northern edge of the swamp and bounced along a beat-up logging trail we had spotted from the air. In another fifteen minutes, we rattled around a bend, left the scrubby brush we had been driving through, and broke into an open stretch of low-growing yellow and orange milkwort flowers. I stared across the field at the wall of dark trees beyond. We had reached the Great Silver.

A pure white egret rose out of the milkwort patch, banked away, and glided along the dark face of the swamp until it disappeared into a weather-whitened stand of dead oak trunks.

The closer the jeep growled, the worse the swamp looked. "I think," Roy said, "it's time for the boots." He braked the jeep, and we pulled on the tough knee-high boots. Roy stuck the compass in his pocket, and we started up again. In another hundred yards, the old road wound around a fallen trunk, and we were in the Great Silver Swamp.

Under the leaves of the weed trees at the swamp's edge, the temperature must have dropped five degrees. I shivered, but Roy didn't laugh. He seemed to feel the same chill, and it wasn't all from the sudden coolness. The road dipped into a sluggish little stream, but we didn't get the jeep that far. It's front wheels began to sink just this side of the water. Roy threw it into reverse and roared back to solid ground. "I'm not taking any chances on that glup," he said. "Looks like from here we walk."

Out in the sunlight as we had raced the jeep across the field, I had felt good in the heat of the Carolina summer. In here, as the engine's last growl was swallowed much too fast by the black-green wall around is, I felt like a little boy caught outside in his pajamas. Who were Roy and I to tackle this whole huge endless swamp with nothing but snakeboots and a surplus compass?

Roy read my face like a set of instruments. "Come on, we're only going in a mile." He clumped across the soft ground, his boots leaving two-inch-deep prints. What could I do? I went right along behind him. We slogged through the mucky little stream, pushed through a stand of some kind of reedy things that left prickly brown burrs on my shirt, then walked across a sudden open area of deep grass. Overhead, the sun managed to send a gleam or two through the arches that hung heavy with Spanish moss. A thousand white butterflies liked it here, and that made me feel better —until I saw my first snake.

We had reached the far side of the butterfly glade and had to step down a two-foot bank into a mud flat. My feet went out from under me halfway down the steep little bank, and I fell backward onto my hands. Something moved under the fingers of my right hand, something thick at first, then tapered. I swung my head, wide-eyed, then froze. The cottonmouth was about three feet long, flat headed, with a thick body. His mottled brownish black markings were hard to make out, which meant he was an old guy. I was glad of that because he was heading away fast, minding his own business. A kid snake might have panicked and taken me on in a hurry.

"Didn't get you, did he?" Roy had come back to see why I'd turned into petrified wood.

"Unh ugnh—"

He figured that meant no and grabbed my arm. "Let's move. We don't want to be in here when it gets dark."

Aha! This *was* getting to him a little, after all. But Roy's need to find that bomber of his was bigger than any snake we were likely to find in here. We slogged across the sucking mud right into some very undelightful saw grass that chopped away at our bare forearms until we rolled down our sleeves. Then the tiny teeth on the darned stuff began to work on our khakis. In five minutes, my right knee was scratched through and the stuff had managed to pull out my shirttail, then stitch me like a sewing machine right above the belt on my left hip.

When we got through that, we rested for a minute or two on a grassy hummock under some tall cypresses. The cuts weren't deep, but they felt like a bad shave with a rusty razor. I shoved my shirt back in and stood on top of the hump.

"How far do you think we've come?"

"About three-quarters of a mile. You spot that tree with the buzzard's nest?"

I looked up through the vines. Some little birds flitted around the tops of a grove of gum trees. "No nest. None of these trees is tall enough, anyway."

"All right, we go on."

I looked at my watch. We had been knocking ourselves out for the better part of an hour already. It was nearly four.

The next part of our little tour was just peachy. You know those special vines that come along out of nowhere, grab you across the belt, and when you try to break them, they're like woven wire with a slimy green coating? Well, that swamp was full of those vines, and they did grab us across the waist, and when we tried to break them. . . . It was maddening. We moved ten feet at a time, ducking and bobbing under and over the tangle like eager rookies on tryout day for a pro football team. My back began to tell me all about its opinion of this nonsense, and my legs above the knees were ready to just plain quit. Then Roy let out a shout that drove a little blue heron right out of his wading place.

I followed his pointing arm. Framed in a hole in the low trees was a tall cypress, gray beards of moss hanging from its broken arms and a buzzard's nest perched right in its top branches.

"That's got to be it, Roy! Now all we have to do it spread out a little. That plane's got to be here somewhere."

We separated, and I pushed through a thick ground web of wild grape vines about a hundred yards to the right of the cypress. Off to my left, I heard Roy's muffled crashing through whatever vines or bushes were on the other side of our marker tree.

Then I found a wall of reeds rising out of a pool of knee-deep water hyacinths. Behind them, I was sure I spotted something solid that had a man-made shape!

"Roy! Roy! Over here!"

My yell knocked a hole in the stillness. A scattering of birds broke from the far side of the hyacinths and whirred deeper into the swamp. A few seconds later, I heard boots crashing through the brush, and Roy pushed into sight.

I pointed into the reeds. "It's in there, Roy!" Excitement was choking me.

"Yeah, I see it. I see it. Good going!" We rushed across the slough, kicking the pulpy hyacinths aside and plunging through the reeds.

Then I couldn't look at Roy. I didn't know what to say to him, so I kept my mouth shut and just stood there. Roy, hands on his hips, walked all around the thing, kicked it a couple of times, then stared up at the huge live oak branches that had hidden it from the air. He finally walked back to me, reached down for a blade of grass, then stood back to gaze at it again.

"Well, the MAD didn't lie, did it? The thing *is* made out of metal. I'd say it's what's left of a tractor-powered saw mill. Must've broken down, so they took the tractor away and left the shed here, and the pulley wheels, and conveyor racks. That old rusty iron roof helped get the MAD agitated, too."

I was at rock bottom. I'd been engraved by saw grass. My clothes were ripped into rags. I slapped my neck and looked at my hand. Like a swarm of miniature Draculas, the mosquitoes were coming out as the sun sank.

Roy's voice sounded as if at least half the world was falling straight toward him. "That sure ends this little trip, doesn't it?"

"I'm sorry, Roy. I really—"

He seemed to get hold of himself again. "I'm just talking about today, kid. We're not finished yet. Come on, let's get out of here."

9

$\mathcal{T}$HE COTTON-SPRAYING OPERATION WAS about to break up until next summer. On top of that, the weather was going sour. The hurricane season was by now well underway. In fact, the Weather Bureau's list was already down through Gracie. So far, the storms had all whirled themselves out in the Caribbean, but we were due for autumn wet weeks whether or not any hurricanes got up this far.

Bouncing back to Derby in the jeep, I asked Roy why he didn't wait until winter knocked the leaves off some of the trees and he could see more of the Great Silver from the air. He'd tried that last year, he told me. But the swamp was thick with oak trees whose leaves turned brown but stayed on until spring, and with evergreen trees and shrubs that didn't lose them at all. "I did spend two weeks down here last winter," he said. "I don't think anybody knows about that except the guy in Columbia I rented the Cessna from. Stayed in a motel there and spent most of every day over the Great Silver. Spent all the money I had. No good. Didn't spot a thing, not even that sawmill we found. No, I'm betting on the MAD."

We phoned Al Derr from Derby, and he hung around the base to put a line of flares along one side of the runway. We didn't get there until an hour after dark. Al knew from our faces that we hadn't found what we were looking for. He helped us carry the MAD to Roy's car and shook his head in sympathy when we told him about the sawmill. We muttered good nights; then Roy and I headed for changes of clothes at Aunt Agony Anthony's.

In the shower, I discovered that I was a mess! A spider web of angry red scratches was spread across my chest and back, and I kept finding nicks and gouges I didn't even remember getting. I got into a clean set of khakis and went on to Moultrie's with Roy. I had to agree with him when he said, "We went into the Great Silver like a couple of amateurs—eager to find what we were looking for, but without any real preparation."

"We had the snake boots and compass," I reminded him.

"Only because the guy in Derby talked us into them," he reminded me right back. "When we go in there again, we're going in equipped."

We didn't get back over the Great Silver until noon the next day because we spent the whole morning going from small town to small town picking up tough whipcord pants, mosquito headgear and repellent, a pair of machetes, waterproof match containers, and other assorted stuff that made me feel as though we were getting ready for a trip up the Amazon. We started the buying spree at Moultrie's, tossed the flashlights into Roy's car, and shoved off for nearby Tarleton, where we bought the jungle clothes and a roll of tennis court marking tape. "You fellers starting a tennis club?" the white-haired owner of Tarleton Sporting Goods had asked.

As we drove out of that little burg, Roy had explained the tape to me. "We might not be lucky enough to find a handy landmark the next time—like that tree with the buzzard's nest near the sawmill. This time, as soon as you hear the MAD screech, you toss out this marking tape. It'll drape over the trees, and we should be able to spot it from the ground when we go in on foot."

We took the jungle gear back to our cabins, loaded the MAD into the Super Cub around eleven-thirty, and took off with the sun beating straight down on us. This weather couldn't last, though. A little tropical storm had stopped wobbling around Cuba, and now it was whirling toward the east coast of Florida. The Weather Bureau decided it was enough of a disturbance on radar to give it a name. The radios in the administration shack at the base and my own transistor began to call it Huldah.

Over the Great Silver, the sun held out until three o'clock. Then an overcast, stretching across the whole sky from east to west, crept up from Georgia, spread its gray umbrella above us, and oozed on northward. It trapped a chill beneath it that told us weather was coming, and it wasn't going to be nice.

We had worked the east-central portion of the swamp for the past two and a half hours. Again, my ears felt as though they'd been boiled under those earphones. You might think ears don't have much feeling in them, but clamp on a headset for a few hours, strain to hear a special signal over the racket of a 125-horse engine, and you'll find out things about your ears that you never knew before. They'll feel like two thumbs just after the hammers hit them. But I couldn't take the earphones off for even an instant. We were moving across the trees about 140 feet per second. In ten seconds, we were covering more than a quarter of a mile.

The swamp flowed below our wheels on and on: trees, shrubs, vines, and saw grass. Choked thickets, then sudden small glades flicked beneath us. The MAD sensor zipped along, a few feet above the tallest trees, its electric impulses reaching out, looking for metal. Looking, looking . . . but finding nothing to interest its eager ears.

I looked at my watch. Three-twenty. Some long afternoon. Roy hunched over the front seat controls, his head moving slowly left to right, back and forth like a patient hawk. Searching, searching—the deep-set eyes squinted against the afternoon light, the mouth a tight straight line.

At three twenty-two, the engine stuttered. Carburetor ice again. Roy reached down and yanked the heat knob. The stuttering got worse, and a cold little thread crawled up my spine. The engine coughed and lost power fast.

Roy joggled the carb heat knob and shouted, "The MAD! Reel it in quick!"

I grabbed the metal cable reel handle and cranked. The cable wound in yard by yard, but with the engine failing fast, the Super Cub was sinking as fast as the cable came in. Maybe even a little faster than I could reel in the MAD. I stuck my head into the slipstream and kept whipping the reel handle around and around.

"Get it up here!" Roy yelled. "I can't hold her."

The nose inched up as he struggled to keep the Cub in the air. I leaned way out and looked down again. The MAD pod was just inches above the trees, and we were still sinking in spite of Roy's efforts to keep some air under us.

A hundred feet of cable to go. We still mushed down, down. . . . The MAD flicked through the tip of a buttonwood. A spray of leaves swirled behind it.

"Felt that," Roy called. "Damaged?"

"MAD went through a treetop," I shouted back. "Doesn't look like it got hurt any."

"How many feet to go?"

"About fifty. I'm winding, I'm winding."

The trees were getting bigger—but so was the sensor pod. I changed hands on the cable reel handle. My right arm felt as if it had just been tenderized with a butcher's mallet, but there wasn't time to worry about details like that. We were nearly on the deck.

The engine hacked and popped hard through the exhaust. That seemed to clear some of the ice out of the air intake. We got a sudden snort of power—but only a snort. The roar faded fast to more hacking and wheezing. As the power dropped, so did we.

A quick look over Roy's shoulder at the compass vibrating in its alcohol told me that we had swung due north, the shortest way out of the Great Silver. I gave the take-up reel its final three whirls. The MAD sensor clunked against the fuselage.

"It's in!" I yelled to Roy.

He nodded and searched the area ahead of us. I decided to leave the pod hanging up against the fuselage. When we crashed, I didn't want that big blue nose smashing into my face. Ahead of us was nothing but scrub swamp. Roy could never put us down there without wrapping the Super Cub into a ball of broken spars and tattered fabric, and us with it.

Then I saw the northern edge of the Great Silver. It seemed miles away, and it was just inching toward us. I was sure we'd never make it.

Roy reached above his head and cut the switch off, then back on. The engine *whammed* like a shotgun, and we picked up a few seconds of power. A very few seconds. The spurt boosted us over a stand of gum trees; then we settled in over the scrub and marshland.

The edge of the swamp was closer now, but it still looked too far away to reach the way we were sinking. Roy back-fired the engine again, shaking out more of the ice. It was a dangerous way to try to clear the engine. I'd heard of planes catching fire from a backfire going the wrong way—back through the carburetor instead of out the exhaust.

I sat up high, straining against the seat belt and shoulder straps, and looked over the Cub's nose. A quarter mile to go. We might actually make it . . .

The engine quit cold! I could see the propeller's shimmer break into individual blades; then it stopped dead. The wind squealing past the open doorway was the only noise now.

Roy punched the starter. The prop flopped over and over on the battery, but the engine wouldn't catch.

"Hang on!" Roy said. "We're going in."

That was obvious, but Roy wasn't going to stop flying until we lay flat on the ground. The swamp ended in a line of sweet gum trees that came at us in a high green wall. Their tops soared past the horizon, standing high against the gray overcast. Too high!

So this was how the search was to end—with Roy and

me and the Super Cub crumpled against the solid line of tree trunks that stood before us like a gigantic picket fence.

Then the wing dipped. We slid off in a flat glide to the right. Was Roy trying to crash-land before we hit the trees? Below us lay a cramped swampy area studded with jagged cypress stumps. That wasn't the best place in the world for a landing, but it was about three percent better than ramming the trees.

My stomach flopped as we reversed suddenly and headed straight for the sweet gums again. What in the . . . ? Then I saw what Roy was trying to do. He'd spotted a hole in the tree line, a gap about thirty feet wide, and he was going to try to squeeze us through there.

The trouble was that the Super Cub's wingspan was thirty-six feet. We wouldn't fit. Then I remembered the old advice to ag pilots: "If you have to land in the woods, head *between* two trees. They'll rip the wings off, but the chances are that the fuselage will stay together. Then you're on your own."

So that was what he had in mind! I braced myself and fought the urge to shut my eyes and bury my head in my arms.

Just before we hit, I got a surprise that showed me how much I had to learn just to call myself a pilot when Roy was around. The trees were only a few feet away, coming at us the way phone poles whiz toward an express train. The Super Cub had about a second and a half still to be called an airplane; then it would be so much junk, and so would we.

In that second, Roy slapped the control stick to his left and fed in top rudder. The Cub tipped sharply but kept going straight ahead—straight through the break in the trees with its wings at enough of an angle to clear them.

We were through! And we were still in one piece! I sagged in the canvas seat. My shirt was soaked and my legs were shaking like car springs on a country road.

We had about four seconds to congratulate ourselves on still being alive. The Cub was moving at sixty miles an hour over a rocky field maybe fifteen feet up, but settling straight for an old stone wall that was big enough and solid enough to stop a tank.

Roy dropped the Cub's nose so fast that half of me was left hanging in space before it could decide to follow the rest of me to the ground.

The wheels hit hard in a grassy flat among the rocks. The landing gear shock cord snapped the nose right up again. We were back in the air, shaking from the impact, wobbling over the wall. The main gear cleared it by three feet. The tail wheel hit the top of it with a bang.

Then we were down a second time, but in a nice level field of weeds without rocks or stumps or anything at all to knock us apart. The Cub didn't roll more than forty feet.

A silence settled all around us. Roy very carefully unbuckled his seat belt and shoulder straps, unfolded out of the cockpit, and walked off beyond the right wing. He looked back the way we had come; looked back at the wall and the line of gum trees and the rocky field between. Then he came back, and I knew that now he felt he could talk without his voice shaking.

"Close thing," he said. "You've got a lot of nerve."

"*I* have! How about you? I just sat and sweated. You did the flying. And *some* flying!"

"Yeah, but you never said a word through the whole thing."

"Because I was too scared to talk."

He gave me that tight little grin of his. "A guy can go one of two ways when he's scared. Either go over the edge into panic, or admit to himself that he's scared but keep his wits about him."

He bent down and inspected the MAD sensor pad, which had been hanging just below the fuselage through all this. "Doesn't look damaged." He straightened and pointed at the small luggage locker behind me. "See if there's a screwdriver in there."

We loosened the cowling fasteners and took a look at the engine. The carburetor intake dripped water.

"Carb ice, all right." Roy fingered the carburetor heater cable, followed it to the firewall, then back to the heat duct from the exhaust. "The bolt securing the cable to the flap valve worked loose and it—"

He bit off his words and bent closer.

"What'd you find?"

"Take a look and tell me what you think."

The little retaining bolt was loose, all right, letting the cable slide through its drilled hole without moving the flap valve at all.

"It's like you said, Roy. The bolt has worked loose."

"Look again."

Then I noticed the gleam of tiny new scratches in the grimy film of the bolt head. And I had missed the obvious: the safety wire was gone.

"Somebody has—"

"That's right," Roy said grimly. "Somebody has loosened that retaining bolt."

The same chill settled over me that I had felt the first day I had driven into South Carolina. Only now it wasn't just a general uneasy feeling that came with the gloomy weather. This was a much more frightening chill. Somebody in particular had fiddled with that carburetor heater cable. Somebody had tried to drop the Super Cub—and us —into the Great Silver Swamp.

10

"Sabotage," Roy said. "No question about it."

I didn't want to believe it. "Maybe the bolt just worked loose by itself."

"Huh uh. Not that particular bolt. And how did the safety wire untwist itself and pull itself out of the bolt head?"

We tightened the bolt in the field north of the Great Silver. Roy made a hair-curling short field takeoff—held the brakes tight, dropped the flaps, ran the engine full up, raised the tail in the slipstream—and we leaped out of there like a scared jaybird.

A half hour later, we walked in from the tie-down line at the base where we had just landed. Al Derr stood in the doorway of the office shack, shading his eyes, wondering what we were doing back so soon.

"Don't say a thing about the carb heat," Roy cautioned. "Letting everybody know about it won't help us find the guy who did it. We'll keep our mouths shut and our eyes open."

Al walked out to meet us. "You guys are back early. What's up?"

"Finished the area we wanted to cover. Decided to knock off until tomorrow."

Al looked at him strangely, and I knew he'd noticed the coldness in Roy's voice. "You want the Super Cub again tomorrow?"

"Yep. But she's been running a little rough. I want to take her in the hangar and tune her up a bit. Take my car to town and bring me back a couple of sandwiches, will you, Greg? I'll be a while."

Al went back into his shack, ready to close up, and Roy said to me, "Leave the MAD here. I'm going to stay with the Cub all night. We're not taking any chances now. Funny thing about this: it couldn't have been Al who goofed up the carburetor heat. But right now, I can't help being suspicious of everybody—except you."

I knew exactly how he felt. Nothing could be the same after that wild forced landing, then our discovery that someone had tried—actually tried to make us crash in the swamp. "So why couldn't it be Al?" I asked.

"Because—well, because it just wouldn't be like him."

"Sabotage wouldn't be like Carl Davis or Eddie Pelton, either, would it? Or like Frank Kingston or Harry Feather. Or like Dobbs Musserman. In fact, I can't picture any of those guys doing it."

"I wonder . . ." Roy said. "I just wonder. Frank and Harry are the guys who could have gotten at the Cub the easiest. They're mechanics—they'd sure know how to gimmick up a carburetor heater, wouldn't they?" He shook his head. "What's the matter with me! None of our guys would pull anything like this. I've known them too long."

"So nobody did it," I said. "The safety wire crawled out, and the bolt just vibrated loose."

"Somebody did it, all right. I wish I didn't have to believe that, but it happened. So we'll watch ourselves."

"And watch everybody else, too."

"I'm afraid so," Roy agreed.

When I got to Moultrie's after a shower and a change of clothes, I was surprised to find The Grizzly, The Beard, and Scoop sitting at a corner table. They were still hanging on, hoping something would develop, I guess. Or maybe it was the slack season in the free-lancing business.

The Grizzly grabbed a spare chair with a huge paw and dragged it to the table. "Sit with us, kid. Might give us another story."

I joined them because it would have looked worse to sit somewhere else. Scoop didn't say anything. He just looked nervous. And The Beard didn't say anything either. His little eyes kept staring at me, like cold glass beads.

"Nearly gave this whole idea up today," The Grizzly said. "Tony here"—he bent his thumb toward The Beard— "about talked us out of sticking around. Then we saw him heading back here himself, so we came along. How come you changed your mind, Tony?"

It was The Beard's turn to shrug. "Wanted some last shots of Blackwater to finish my file."

Scoop put in with his high-pitched voice, "I can tell by looking at Stewart that they didn't find anything today, either."

The Grizzly chuckled and nudged me with his lumpish elbow. "Come on, kid. You've had your fun with us. Why don't you admit that Burnette's just been suckering the press? He's got his name around, got some pictures printed. What more does he want?"

Moultrie stood over me with his hands on his hips, his butcher's apron as crusty as ever. "What'll it be, gents?"

I ordered a rubber steak sandwich and coffee and turned back to The Grizzly. "All we want," I said, "is to find that—"

"—bomber in the swamp," The Grizzly finished for me. "Brother, you'll believe anything, won't you? What'll it take to stop you?"

The way he said that made me think some pretty ugly thoughts, but they were nonsense, of course. Why would a free-lance writer care about that ghost bomber of Roy's, except as a possible story sale?

They had been half finished with their supper when I sat down. It wasn't hard to stall around until they hit the road for Charleston. Then I got Roy's sandwiches and a milk bottle of coffee and drove back to the base.

I wanted to stay with Roy, but he shooed me out of there. "No reason for both of us to sleep on the hangar floor," he said. "Just be back here before it gets light."

So I returned to Blackwater, and from my little transistor radio in the cabin, I learned that Hurricane Huldah was a big threat now. She had rolled out of the Atlantic, coming ashore just north of Miami, then crashed across southern Florida. Out in the Gulf of Mexico, she had swung north and was expected to hit the Florida Panhandle in about three hours.

I got out to the base before dawn. Roy reported that he hadn't seen or heard anything—"Unless you consider Harry Feather coming back here for some wrenches around midnight. Said a water pipe had let go in the house where he rents a room, and the owner didn't have the tools to fix it."

"Does that sound a little strange?" I asked.

"Maybe. Maybe not. We'll keep an eye on him."

"Along with everybody else."

Roy had put a new safety wire on the carb heat bolt and had spent a lot of his time last night inspecting every inch of the Super Cub that he could get at. We rolled the big hangar doors open and pushed the plane into the chilly blackness of early morning.

In the rear seat, I hunched over the cold nose of the MAD sensor. Roy cranked her up, and we taxied to the closest end of the old runway. There wasn't any wind at all. He booted the tail around, gunned the engine, and we roared out of the base just as first light began to melt away the darkness.

I knew that Roy had spent all night with the plane, that he hadn't been out of sight of it for even a minute. Yet I couldn't relax. Maybe the guy who had fooled with the carb heat had been trickier than we thought. Maybe he had done something more under the cowling that would catch up with us over the Great Silver again this morning. . . . Maybe he'd put something in the fuselage where it couldn't be checked unless we stripped off the fabric . . .

A whole string of maybes haunted me all the way to the swamp, but Roy didn't seem to suffer from such doubts at all. He pulled his own county plat map out of his knee pocket and strapped it to his thigh, and we began the search routine. We swung over the Great Silver from the northwest and waltzed back and forth in flat esses until Roy found the quadrant we had been searching when the engine picked up yesterday's load of ice. Then he lined up due west on the compass. I let down the MAD on its two hundred feet of thin cable, and the day began.

At nine o'clock, we were starting a new quadrant. I was

beginning to feel the fact that I hadn't had much sleep last night. The same dream kept waking me up. First Carl Davis's blond crewcut head was bending over the Cub's engine, and he had some kind of hatchet or something in his big hands. Then it was stumpy little Eddie Pelton. Then Frank Kingston, like a tall, shaggy crow, and bullet-headed Harry Feather, both with chisels that they kept jabbing under the cowling. I had yelled at them, and that woke me up the first time. Then it was Al Derr himself, then even The Grizzly, The Beard, and Scoop, until I was sick of the whole dream. The fourth time my eyes flew open, I had stayed awake and listened to hurricane reports on the radio . . .

Roy was yelling something at me and pointing south with his thumb. I lifted one earphone. ". . . weather. Look over there."

I followed the thumb. The horizon to the south looked like muddy water in a Pennsylvania coal town—gray-black, and thick with trouble.

"Huldah?" I yelled back.

"Hem of her skirt." The air was beginning to get rocks in it. We jounced hard. "Looks like we'd better—"

At that instant, the earphones squealed loud and clear. Without any thought at all, my right arm swung sideways, and the fat roll of tennis court tape flew through the door opening. I craned my neck around the opening. Behind us, the roll bloomed into a white ribbon, twisted in the air, then draped itself over a big cypress, by now a quarter of a mile behind us.

Roy swung the nose around, and we headed back toward the marker. The tangle of tape flicked beneath us, and the MAD howled again. We turned back, and a third sweep told us that whatever we had found lay about a quarter of a mile east of the tree where the tape had landed. We made a slow circle of the area, a fairly open marsh dotted with hummocks—islands of trees and brush that had grown on ground a few feet higher than the flood level during wet seasons.

Roy signaled, and I reeled in the MAD cable. When I lifted the sensor pod into the cockpit and set it on end between my knees, he bent us out of our holding circle, banked around tightly, throttled back, and we passed low over the area that had gotten the MAD interested. It was disappointing. How could something the size of a bomber hide among little islands of vegetation in the flat open marsh? The islands were covered with wild grape vines and other assorted crawly-type plants. Trees jutted out of them, big cypresses and sweet gums, trailing skirts of Spanish moss.

All around the strange vine-covered humps was a waist-high sea of saw grass, great for snakes and tigers . . . and my imagination was getting out of hand.

I was being pulled two ways at once. I wanted to see what kind of sawmill we'd found this time, but I wasn't too eager to plow through that crazy swamp again. I still wore the scars from the last safari.

Roy throttled back, and in the engine lull he said, "I got a feeling this time. Got a feeling."

The way he said it told me I was going in there with him, no matter how miserable it was going to be.

He gave the engine a long burst of power, then eased off again. "We've got to get back in here in a hurry, from the look of that sky."

I stared south. The sky was blue-black down at its edge, so dark I could barely see where it ended and the horizon began.

The engine drummed again, but we didn't head east

111

toward Blackwater. Roy began working us northward in wide swings. I realized he was looking for the quickest route to get back here on the ground.

He pointed down and to the right. I took a look, spotted a fair-sized creek wandering beneath overhanging branches, and I knew what he was thinking. We marked our maps, then followed the stream north. It widened and finally came out the northern edge of the Great Silver about fifty feet across and flowing no faster than maple syrup on a cold day. Looked about the same, too. Three miles farther on, now in open country, it made a wide eastern swing to go around some high ground, and it passed within half a mile of a narrow dirt road.

That was what we needed. Roy banked east, and we landed at the base well before noon.

I jumped out as soon as we stopped rolling, but Roy grabbed my arm. "Hold it a minute. Don't say anything to anybody. I'll do the talking. I don't want to get hung up on a false alarm like we were before. We'll take it nice and easy, load our swamp gear into my car, and drive right to Derby."

"Derby?"

"We can borrow Art Ford's jeep again. And I noticed Crimmins Hardware had outboards for rent to fishermen. Use them on the Wateree River, I guess. I just want to do it all quietly. If we flop, we flop. If we find something, then we can talk about it afterwards."

I looked straight at him. "The way things are shaping up, we'd better find something, Roy."

"Yeah," he said. "That's sure the way it's shaping up."

Al Derr ambled over from the hangar as we loaded the MAD into Roy's car. "Back pretty early."

"Weather's getting awful thick," Roy said truthfully. And

I could tell that he was trying to keep excitement out of his voice. "Air's full of lumps."

"Harry tells me you were still in the hangar with the Club around midnight. Anything wrong?"

"Decided to give her a real good checkout, Al. We've been flying her pretty hard."

"Uh huh. Well, I think she'll get a rest over the next few days. Huldah flooded out Pensacola two hours ago, and she's veered northeast. Expected to hit Charleston sometime tonight. I'll have to have the boys put all the ships in the hangar. Can't take any chances with leaving them tied down outside."

"You want a hand?" Roy asked, his face blank. My heart twitched. We'd be here an hour, pushing and shoving Pawnees around to fit them all into the maintenance hangar.

"We could use a couple of extra—" Al looked at Roy closely and stopped. Then he said, in a whole new voice, "Roy, we been pretty close for the past couple of years. I know you better'n you think. You've found something out there, haven't you? Not another sawmill this time?"

Roy's face didn't change.

"O.K.," Al said. "If it's gotta be that way. There are enough of us here to get the planes under cover. Shove off, you two."

Dressed for the job this time, we got to the Derby Airport just before one o'clock, wolfed down quick hamburgers, and bounced off in Art Ford's jeep for the hardware store. On the way, I said, "I'm not so sure I like the way Ford gave this to us so fast and without asking any questions at all."

"What bothered me more," Roy said thoughtfully, "was that he went to the phone just as we were driving out of there."

I hadn't noticed that, and I wasn't too glad Roy had told me about it. "Maybe he was calling his insurance agent," I said, but it didn't come out very funny.

"Word got around that we're working the search out of Derby. Maybe Ford was calling somebody who paid him to call if we showed up."

"Some guy who loosens carburetor heater bolts for a hobby?"

We pulled into the Crimmins Hardware Store parking lot a couple of minutes later, then had a tough time talking old man Crimmins into postponing his anti-hurricane window taping long enough to do business.

At ten minutes to two, we rolled out of the parking lot, towing an eleven-foot aluminum fishing boat with a compact outboard motor. The rig was mounted on a two-wheeled trailer.

It took us a good hour to find the dirt road we'd spotted from the air; then we bounced along its narrow rutted surface for another fifteen minutes before we found the stretch that ran near the creek.

Roy squeaked the jeep to a halt, and we looked down the long slope to the stream. The sky was darkening fast beyond the Great Silver, which we could see in the hazy distance, a great olive-colored smear across the horizon beneath the oily clouds.

"I think we can work the jeep right down to the creek," Roy said. "Hang on. This could be a rough ride."

Rough was an understatement. We bounced from rock to rock, the metal boat thundering along behind us, but we made it to the creek in just two pieces, the jeep and the trailer-boat rig. Roy pulled up along a skinny stretch of beach, and we manhandled the boat into the water.

I climbed aboard, and Roy passed me the stuff out of the

back of the jeep: the items we had gathered after our first tangle with the Great Silver. We had stuffed it into two backpacks, which I lay in the bottom of the boat.

Roy snapped a canvas cover in place over the open jeep and stepped into the boat with me. We pushed away from the bank with one of the aluminum emergency oars that were clipped below the gunwales. Roy lowered the motor into running position and shoved the retaining pin in place. He set the throttle, hit the primer plunger a couple of whacks, and yanked the nylon starter lanyard.

The motor coughed blue, then caught and purred quietly. Roy guided us into midstream. A swirl of current slapped the bow back toward shore, but Roy countered with a quick move of the tiller. We cruised around a wide bend, lost sight of the jeep, and headed upstream toward the Great Silver Swamp.

11

*I*T'S A CALCULATED RISK," ROY HAD SAID BACK in Blackwater. "After a big storm, we wouldn't be able to get near the Great Silver on foot for days. That tape marker we dropped will be somewhere in Virginia. The MAD's daddy wants his stuff back for a military contract test, and his lawyer will be on our necks in a day or two with all kinds of legal hand-tying. We've got six, seven hours before Huldah gets really nasty. Maybe she'll even veer off in another direction. If we're quick about it, we can be in and out of the Great Silver before dark."

Of course, what he had really meant was that nothing on earth could hold him back now. He felt that he was too close to proving what actually had happened in the hazy South Carolina sky thirty years ago to slow down now.

Could we actually get in and out of the Great Silver by daylight? We had used up a couple of hours already, getting our stuff together, borrowing the jeep, renting the boat, finding the stream, and launching ourselves into its sluggish current.

As the motor drummed us upstream toward the reaching arms of the swamp, I couldn't get out of my mind the fact that somebody else was more than just interested in what we were up to. He had sabotaged us once, and there was no reason to think that he wouldn't do it again if he had the chance.

But why? What could possibly be in the Great Silver that would have driven somebody to try to dump us into the swamp yesterday? And who could the saboteur be? Roy and I had talked over the possibilities, and we had come up with nothing that seemed to make any sense.

As the boat pushed through the creek that oozed out of the Great Silver Swamp, I let my imagination wander a little. How about those hard-nosed farmers I'd run into the first day I had come down here? Could big Herm or Ralphie have some strange secret hidden deep in the swamp that they didn't want uncovered? They knew about car and tractor engines. Could they know about the carburetor heat problem in a small airplane engine?

Behind me, Roy pushed the outboard engine throttle up a notch, and the bow lifted. We came out of the low hills and began to cross the open fields north of the Great Silver. The lowering sky spread a gloomy curtain over the swamp. Its light was greenish, making the grass and weeds brighter than they should be and the shadows blacker. We cut through some swamp debris—twigs and battered green leaves drifting out of the Great Silver to ride the stream down to the Wateree, then eastward out to sea.

117

Roy said, "Must have been a hard rain around here last night. A small storm traveling ahead of Huldah, I guess. Tore this stuff right off the trees. Could get pretty mucky in there."

From my hard seat in the middle of the boat, I watched the tree line of the swamp move toward us and grow taller. Far to the south, the sky flashed greenish white. A while later, thunder mumbled like a hibernating bear who was going to be mean when he finally woke up all the way.

We swung around an old cypress stump that stuck out of the water like a black broken tooth, scraped over a sunken log, and the swamp closed around us. I looked back past Roy and watched the break through which we had come in grow smaller. Then Roy swung the tiller to follow a bend in the stream, and the opening disappeared.

Out in the open, the motor had seemed quiet. Now its racket bounced off the tree trunks. We moved along in our own wave of noise that scared egrets out of the weeds along the creek banks. We heard their cries above the popping as they flapped away, white against the dark trees.

I looked through the branches that closed above us to make a tunnel over the stream. Through the leaves, the sky was gunmetal gray. Lightning flared again, but the thunder was drowned in the hammering of the outboard.

Roy checked his watch. He had estimated our speed and was working out where we were on his map. I pulled out my own map and made a private guess. It was close. He shut off the engine fifteen seconds before I figured he would.

The buzz-sawing engine noise seemed to sink right into the water. We drifted in dead silence. It was eerie—as if I had suddenly gone stone deaf. There wasn't a frog croak or a bug buzz or a single bird call.

I shook my head and dug my finger in an ear, and Roy

said, "I feel the same way. It's like we're the only things alive in here." Even his voice was hushed.

He bent the tiller hard. The bow nudged the right bank of the stream, and I stepped ashore in three inches of sucking mud. Roy clumped in from the stern, and together we hauled the metal boat up on the foot-high bank. Then he tied the bow rope to a three-inch willow tree in a closely bunched group of four. "Just to be doubly sure," he said. "No telling how high the water could rise across these flats."

We strapped the equipment packs in place high on our backs. Roy studied the county plat map and pulled out his compass. "Due west from here, I'd say. Let's move."

As if that were some kind of secret signal, the mosquitoes hit us in whining clouds. It took us nearly five minutes to get the packs off, slap on insect repellent, and pull on our foldable mosquito net headgear.

We finally set out looking like two amateur beekeepers, but by now it would take more than that to strike us funny. Huldah's probing edge, reaching far north of the storm center, soared blackly above us. The mutterings to the south seemed to shake a thin gray mist out of the ground like wispy smoke. It curled around our boots and stirred aside as we pushed into the woods.

A hundred yards from the stream, the forest opened into a mushy area that was waist-deep in ferns. Then the trees closed in again, and whip-like sapling branches flew back as Roy passed. One of the slaps knocked my mosquito netting sideways. I walked right into a tree while I struggled to straighten the darned thing out again.

A mosquito worked its way up my sleeve and stabbed my upper arm. In less than a minute, I had a welt that I could feel right through my heavy shirt. It hurt like a boil. These swamp mosquitoes could put the ordinary Pennsylvania variety to shame.

The solid woods began to break into islands of trees and brush, anchored in a sea of waist-high saw grass. The long spears were rooted in three inches of glup as solid as chocolate pudding. We had to slow down to keep from falling into the stuff.

With fewer trees, it was lighter here, but I could see that the day was really going fast now. Unless we found what we were looking for in the next few minutes, we would never get back even to the stream before dark, let alone get all the way out of the Great Silver.

A small dark shape whizzed between us and then was gone. Another flicked past my ear, and I heard a high-pitched squeak. "Bats," Roy said. "They're after the mosquitoes."

I ducked as another skittered just above my head. "I hope their radar is good."

We slogged around a brush-choked hummock, and I crashed right into Roy, who had stopped to study the compass again. "Stay on the ball," he snapped. "We ought to be almost there."

It didn't seem worthwhile to tell him that I'd been watching a stick five feet to our left turn into the biggest water snake I'd ever seen in my life. The snake had gotten out of there in a hurry, essing away through the saw grass, making for a huge nearby hummock, overgrown with a thick mat of flowering vines.

"Start checking the trees for that tennis court tape," Roy said. "Should be around here someplace."

The treetops were black against the gray clouds. We moved slowly through the muck, pushing the tallest saw grass aside with our arms, hands bent inward, away from the tough little teeth that edged the blades.

In ten minutes of eyestrain, we had found a buzzard's nest, a fish hawk who watched us closely as we studied the trees—but no marking tape. We had wandered among the tree islands, and if we hadn't had the compass, we wouldn't have had the remotest idea where to head next. The mosquitoes had found a lot of ways to get at me by now, and I was itching everywhere. Something was sticking my legs with little needles, and I was half blind with perspiration, although chills jittered along my spine in that weird silence that gripped the Great Silver.

Then the sun broke through the rolling clouds to the west. It was the last flare of warmth before Huldah slammed her clammy fist across the Carolinas. The golden light moved fast across our section of the Great Silver Swamp as the cloud cover raced northward. The sunlight washed the trees around us, and their leaves seemed to be cast in green metal. We stopped. The wilderness was a huge sculpture. Every blade of grass was edged with gold. Water droplets glittered like diamonds. The gnarled tree trunks were blackened iron.

And less than a quarter mile southwest, riding high on the upreaching branches of a towering cypress, a tangled ribbon gleamed chalk-white against the gunmetal sky.

"Roy!" My voice chopped the stillness apart. "Over there —our marker!"

We plunged around two smaller clusters of trees before we reached the hummock where the cypress towered over a shorter stand of buttonwoods. In its top branches hung our tennis court tape. No doubt about it.

Roy looked back the way we had come. "Let's see, now.

We were flying west. You dropped the tape maybe two or three seconds after the MAD reacted. So what we're looking for should be about five hundred feet east of here."

"How come we haven't found it already? We walked in here from the east."

"It's been hidden for nearly thirty years. I don't think we're just going to stumble into it. We'll spread out a hundred yards apart. Then we'll move back eastward, parallel to each other. That way, we ought to be able to cover an area about an eighth of a mile wide if we keep our eyes open."

He slogged off to the south, and I plodded north, my boots going *squish squish* every time I pulled up a foot to take another step.

Roy whistled and I looked around. He figured we were far enough apart. I could see his head and shoulders above the saw grass. He looked shapeless in his mosquito-proof head covering and with the lumpy pack strapped to his back. And he looked kind of helpless, too, hunched in the tall grass under the overhanging swamp trees. We began to walk east.

The plan was hopeless, I decided after ten minutes of plowing back through the marsh of rasp-edged grass. The tree- and vine-covered islands couldn't hide a thing but brush and weeds. I studied each hummock as I moved past, and daylight showed through from the other side. Why was I out here in this miserable place, scratching bites, feeling an unknown something picking at my legs, waiting for Huldah to roll in like a tidal wave? I wanted to race back to the boat, fire up the engine, and get the heck out of here. It was the only sensible—

I stopped and squinted at the thick hummock fifty yards to my right. It was the same tree island that I'd seen the big water snake head for when I'd passed here the first time. That cluster of trees and scrub wasn't like the others. It seemed much more dense—almost solid, in fact. I walked closer.

The tree island was about three acres of closely woven vines, sprinkled with waxy white flowers like a swarm of butterflies waiting for the right moment to take off. The largest trees, five of them, soared a good sixty feet up at one edge of the hummock. Smaller trees clustered around their thick bases. The vines had blanketed the whole island with a solid mat of bark-covered main stems as thick as my wrist. Webs of bright green tendrils wound through the mess, knitting it even tighter.

I kicked at a vine stem and turned away. Ridiculous to think anything could be in this isolated hummock, standing alone in the marsh. Then something caught my eye—a stump. It was a couple hundred feet east of the hummock, rotted low to the ground; an old stump, and not particularly interesting—except that maybe a hundred yards beyond it was a group of three more old stumps. And all three had been broken off twenty feet from the ground.

My heart bumped hard. I pushed through the sawgrass farther east. Beyond them, weed trees blocked my line of sight.

I shoved off through the marsh, moving out to get a look past the stand of weed trees. When I had worked out maybe two hundred feet, I spotted what I was looking for. I didn't believe it, but there it was.

An old cypress trunk stood back there a quarter of a mile, its dead wood silvery against the low clouds. Its top had broken off years ago. Thirty years ago? I shouted for Roy, and a few minutes later, he crashed into sight through the heavy grass.

"It's the stump, Roy! I think the trees got knocked down. There are three back there and another—"

"Whoa!" Roy said. "Slow down. You're not making a heck of a lot of sense. Take it slow and easy."

He was right. I was so excited, I was almost babbling. I took a deep breath; then I pointed at the stump nearest the hummock. "First I spotted that. Then I noticed that group of three more stumps farther east, much taller, like all three had been broken off higher up. Now look back there."

His eyes followed my arm. "You see that cypress? It looks like the top was clipped off. They're all in line with each other, and with the hummock. It's as if—"

"Yeah! As if something came in here and chopped those trees off in a descending line."

"And it headed right into that big tree island," I said. My throat went dry.

Roy stared at the hummock; then he said, "Get out your machete." His voice was tight with the excitement he was trying to hold down.

Lightning knifed out of the low clouds and bulleted into the swamp to the south. Its electric white flare silhouetted the black hummock. The thunder shook the mush under our feet not many seconds later. Huldah was getting too close.

In the hush following the thunder roll, I thought I heard an odd sound—the distant drumming of a motor. It faded, then was gone.

"Did you hear that, Roy? Sounded like an engine."

He listened. "Nobody'd be flying this close to a hurricane. Must've been wind."

But it hadn't sounded like an airplane.

"Get that machete," Roy ordered. "We're going to take a look under those vines."

A blast of cold wind flattened the saw grass. The swamp's heat closed in behind it again, but I knew we had just felt the first breath of Huldah.

12

THE FIRST VINE I TOOK A CUT AT WAS AS tough as hard rubber. The heavy machete bounded back and nearly got me across the knee.

"Use more of an angle," Roy suggested. I swung from higher up. The blade bit in deep, and whitish sap dripped from the lower end of the cut. I was through the heavy vine in five swings. Roy was making headway, too. In a few more minutes, we had worked five or six feet into the heavy mat. A sliced stem flew back from Roy's downchop and slapped my arm. My own machete slipped out of my fingers and bounced away into the deeper tangle.

We heard a clank!

"Rock, maybe?"

"Sounded more like metal on metal," I said. My throat was suddenly so tight that the words came out in a croak.

Roy stared at me. Then he began to chop like a threshing machine. The vines fell away in a storm of flying leaves and chips. Together we ducked into the big hole we had made and were beneath the thick canopy of vegetation that covered the hummock. We ripped off our mosquito gear and stared.

One of the big twin rudders was close enough for me to touch. I edged around the huge metal oval. The fat fuselage had broken its back when the bomber had bellied in, and the nose was flattened against the tree trunks at the edge of the hummock. The great wings, set high on the fuselage, had cracked at their roots, and the outer sections had smashed into wreckage.

Roy said slowly, "After all these years . . . all these years . . ." His voice broke and he turned away.

My heart was thundering in my ears. *Here it was!* The ghost plane of Blackwater. Right in front of us.

Roy stood as though frozen, his hands at his sides, his eyes squinting through the poor light under the vine mat. Then he snapped himself out of it.

"I've got to take a look in there." As he moved toward the old relic, Huldah rumbled, and something inside the hulk vibrated.

I followed him to the left waist window. He ran his fingers along the lower edge. "You can still see the char where it blew out. I went right through here, head first."

He bent to look beneath the fuselage. "Bottom hatch is flat against the ground. Top hatch is way up front and covered with vines. This is the easiest way in, right here."

The bottom of the window was four or five feet from the ground. I climbed in after Roy, and we fumbled in our packs for our flashlights. Lightning flamed bright white, a giant flashbulb going off. Again. And again. And each blinding flare burned an image into my eyes that I knew had to be some kind of freak of my imagination.

I thought I saw a skull, bone-white, in a corner of the boxcar-sized fuselage waist.

In the middle of the crash of thunder that followed, Roy clicked on his flashlight. When he did, I dropped mine. He swung his light to my face.

"I don't know what you expected, Greg. I've always said there probably were four guys still aboard when she crashed."

There wasn't just one skeleton in here with us. There were two.

"One of them must have been Bob Sheckler, the flight engineer," Roy said, moving forward past the rusted ball turret. "The other was Fussy Gilfus. He was the radio operator."

I found my light and snapped it on. Roy stood over the two skeletons.

All the clothing had rotted away, even the shoes. He moved his light around. Then he crouched between the two groups of tumbled bones. His hands reached out twice. "Dogtags." He scraped the green off the little brass wafers with the edge of his machete blade and held them in his flashlight's beam. "Yeah. Fussy and Bob."

The identification tags seemed to have more effect on Roy than our discovery of the skeletons in the first place. He hunched there on the broken flooring of the old bomber, his elbows on his knees and his hands hanging between them.

"Fussy and Bob . . ." His voice was distant. I knew his thoughts had gone way back to that day thirty years ago when this corroded old wreck had been a shiny new four-engined bomber roaring toward the Great Silver. Lightning exploded again, and the wham of thunder an instant later told us that Huldah was coming like a giant hammer on the downswing. "We'd better get out of here in a hurry, Roy."

"Uh?" He looked at me blankly. Then he got hold of himself. "Yeah, yeah, you're right. I've got to check up forward; then we'll get moving."

I didn't want to budge anywhere except back out that window, but I forced myself to scramble after him. We edged between the skeletons and ducked into the little opening in the bulkhead they lay against.

We were in the bomb bay, a huge empty tunnel with a central catwalk at the bottom of some narrow V-shaped supports. The big corrugated metal doors had buckled in the crash, but not too badly. Rather than squeeze through the supports, as the crew members had done in flight, we stepped off the catwalk and crunched forward on the bomb bay doors. The old metal sagged beneath our feet like moldy cardboard. Aluminum alloy doesn't rust, but it does develop a white crust that amounts to the same thing over a much longer time.

Roy stopped at the forward end of the bomb bay, and his hands began to explore the corroded tubes and pipes overhead. I couldn't figure out what was so interesting up there, but suddenly he grunted, and his eyes seemed to light up in the beam of my flash. "Well! This has got to be it!"

"What—"

Huldah flashed and roared right over my question. A wind blast shook the hummock. "Later," Roy said, sticking something in his pocket. "We've got to be quick now. The storm's rolling in too fast."

I followed him through the opening in the front end of

the bomb storage section. The fuselage was split-level here. A low passageway led off to the right.

"That goes into the navigator's compartment up forward, then to the nose turret."

The crash had telescoped the nose badly, though, and the passage was blocked with old twisted metal. Roy poked his flashlight toward the debris and shook his head. "What's left of Joe Pirelli is up there, I guess."

The upper level of the forward section had a small room just ahead of the bomb bay. "The flight deck," Roy said. We boosted ourselves up on the rotting second-level floor. "Radio operator sat up here on the right when he had business to attend to. Fussy was riding in the waist with Sheckler until the next radio check, I guess."

The right side of the flight deck was a tumbled pile of electrical-looking metal boxes. A vine had snaked through them, then died when the thick mat over the bomber had completely cut off sunlight. "Tuning units for the big liaison radio," Roy said. "They were stored in brackets against the forward bomb bay bulkhead. Crash broke them loose. Broke something else loose, too. Look at that."

His flashlight beam went right through a fuselage hole above our heads and turned the foliage silver in the vine cover that had closed over it. "The upper turret tore out of there when the plane hit. An old B-24 trick. Look there."

He had lowered the flashlight, and I saw that the big gun turret had fallen forward into the pilot's compartment and slammed into the throttle console between the two seats.

I saw more than that. In the co-pilot's chair, a third skeleton had tumbled over the control column.

"Art Rowan," Roy said almost in a whisper. "Happened quick, I guess. In fact, the explosion in the air could have done it. I doubt if anybody was alive when the plane hit."

130

"How come it didn't turn into one big fireball?" I asked. "You were originally heading out over the Atlantic, weren't you? The gas tanks must have been almost full."

"I'd guess that she came down in a long glide, flaming inside from the gas leak, hit in the marsh, and raised such a huge fan of water that it put the fire out and cushioned the impact at the same time. It happened during the wet season. Then the wreck slid under the foliage in this hummock. It would have come right out again except for that stand of big trees. They were as solid as iron, and the bomber had probably lost a lot of momentum by the time it hit them. They stopped her, and here she lay, covered by the vine mat. No wonder the Air Force search planes couldn't spot anything. If they'd—"

He cut off his words. There was a train coming. A *train?* The distant rumble did sound like a fast freight crashing toward us, but we knew what it really was. We had taken too much time. Huldah was going to make us pay for that.

"Out!" Roy said. "Quick!"

We raced back through the bomb bay, clattered into the waist section, and tumbled through the window. Daylight had almost completely gone. We needed our flashlights to find the opening we had chopped in the vines.

The light was a little better outside in the marsh. Other tree islands were black lumps against the gray of the saw grass. We headed east at a fast trot, our backpacks bumping as we ran.

A wind blast caught me. My feet tangled, and I sprawled in the rasping grass. A blade of the stuff opened a nasty cut on my cheek as I went down.

But there was no time to worry about little things like that. Roy grabbed my arm, hoisted me to my feet, and we got going again.

He was shining his light into his hand as he ran, checking the compass. Lightning froze him against the black trees ahead like a strobe flash. Thunder shook the jellied ground that sucked at my boots with every step. It seemed as if the Great Silver were trying to hold us in there now that we had discovered its secret.

We reached the dense woods that lay between the marsh and the stream. The going was a little easier underfoot here, but sapling branches whipped my face like hot wires as I stumbled after Roy.

A rain shower hit us. We heard it pounding hard through the trees to our right; then the sky opened over us. The drops were as big as peas, and they popped as they slammed into leaves around us. In less than half a minute, we were soaked through.

The shower passed, just a brief preview of wilder things to come. To the south, the freight train roared louder. Our flashlights' pencil beams were swallowed in huge flares of lightning. Thunder exploded right on top of us. Jagged white spears flashed into the trees to our right, and orange flames glowed against the night as a dead tree caught fire.

Then we almost fell into the stream. It had already risen several coffee-colored inches and was widening into the woods. We played our lights along the creek bank; then lightning turned the woods into blinding daylight.

"Up there about a hundred yards!" Roy shouted. "I saw the four willow trees."

We plunged upstream along the west bank. I waited for our boat to come into sight among the reeds along the edge of the creek. It never did. I stood panting by the willows, not wanting to believe what had happened. "Washed away," I said. "The water rose a lot faster than—"

"No," Roy broke in, "it didn't wash away. Not with the

132

knot I put in that rope. Somebody followed us in here and took our boat back out. That's what you heard just as we began to cut through the vines at the hummock."

I leaned against one of the willows, my legs like gelatin. First the carburetor heat, now the boat. "What can we do? We can't stay *here* all night."

"That's the truth. This stream has come up two more inches while we've been standing here. The way it's already raining back in the swamp, this whole area can be under five or six feet of water in an hour or so."

The wind hit like a moving wall. Behind it came that roaring train noise. Then it was right on top of us. A solid screen of rain rolled across the woods, chewing up the surface of the creek as it swallowed us.

"Back to the plane!" Roy yelled. "It's on the highest spot around here."

I was scared enough not to think about the hard pull back to the hummock. I ran into a tree in the woods, and it knocked me flat and left a big bruise over my left eye. Then I tripped over two logs that turned out to be Roy's legs. He'd fallen just ahead of me. We helped each other up and stumbled on through the wind-whipped waterfall.

At first, the woods seemed to get soggier underfoot; then my boots were splashing through a couple of inches of water. Then it was really hard going through nearly a foot of it. The Great Silver was flooding fast.

Just as I felt I couldn't go more than six feet farther— the distance I'd cover when I fell flat on my face—we broke out into the marsh. Now it had become a true swamp. Each lightning flare showed us a knee-deep sea with grass sticking out of it and great sheets of rain smashing across its surface.

We plunged into it. The water filled our boots and tried to hold us back as we plunged toward the high ground of the hummock. We played our waterproof flashlights ahead of us. We weren't alone in that rising water. A dozen snakes were swimming in all directions, looking for something solid to rest on. Some larger animal paddled across our path; an otter, I guessed. He seemed a lot more at home in the water than we did.

In a few more minutes, the depth had reached a good three feet. We couldn't lift our legs free now, and we shoved forward against the water's weight like divers on the floor of the ocean. I wondered how long a guy could go on like this. Then I discovered how you do it. You forget everything but the next step—just the next step. Make it, then begin to worry about the next one.

Then Roy hollered, "There! There it is!" And we had found our tree island. We floundered to the edge of the vine mat, found the hole we had chopped in it, and stumbled through.

For a long time, we just leaned against the old fuselage, not able to move or even speak. The rain beat hard on the vines above us, and water came through in a thousand steady streams. The island grew smaller and began to melt into muck under our boots.

"Come on," Roy ordered. "We've got to get inside."

I found two or three ounces of strength somewhere, and I managed to climb through the waist window with Roy boosting me from outside. Then I helped drag him through, and we lay on the almost dry floor, wheezing like two old gaffers who had just run a hundred-yard dash for their retirement checks.

When I was finally able to sit up, Roy had a dandy suggestion. "There's nothing in here to build a fire with, but we ought to wring out these soaked clothes."

It was while I was doing that cold exercise that I discovered what had been picking my legs. They were dark lumps like snails without shells, and they were happily sucking my blood. I jumped as if I'd stepped into a wasp nest.

"Just leeches," Roy said. "Calm down and pick them off. They won't hurt you any more than they have already, which isn't much."

Sitting in the waist compartment of an old crashed bomber in clammy clothes with two skeletons in one of the Carolinas' biggest swamps isn't the best way to spend a night. Rain pelted across the hummock in great solid sheets. Wind blasts shook the whole island, came right through the vine mat, and howled through chinks and cracks in the old wreckage like a sour pipe organ.

Sometime during the night, one of the big trees that had stood so long at the edge of the hummock broke against the wall of wind, its trunk shattering like a cannon blast. It fell across the right wing, and the impact knocked me away from the fuselage wall.

I finally did manage to fall asleep. I didn't know that was possible or even that I had until I woke up cramped in a tight ball, my arms locked around my knees. Milky gray light had crept into the old fuselage. Across from me, Roy stood with his machete drawn back high over his shoulder. His arm swept forward. The heavy blade whirled toward me and clanged on the metal floor beside my right hip.

I rolled away from it, scared and furious at the same time. Had he gone out of his mind during the night? Was the shock of actually finding his old crew too much for him?

I scrambled to my feet, every muscle in my legs fighting against me. "What are you trying—"

"Take a look where you were sitting," Roy said.

The cottonmouth, a good four feet long, was skittering away through a jagged hole in the floor.

"He decided it would be better in here, too," Roy said. "Can't blame him really. Probably slept there next to you most of the night. And he's not the only company we have. Check outside."

I wobbled over to the window and looked. Beneath the vine mat, water had crept in to make the island about half the size it had been yesterday. And on the remaining land, the hummock was crawling with cottonmouths and other thick black water snakes. Cringing beneath shrubs were little dark brown marsh rabbits, some kind of ratlike animal, and a few other little four-legged things I couldn't identify at the moment. Almost beneath my feet, I heard a dry vibration.

"Rattlesnake," Roy said. "Under the fuselage. This wild life is the usual result of a flood in areas like this. They're after the same thing we are: high ground. All the hummocks are like zoos by now."

"How are we going to get off this island? I don't much want to plow through that menagerie, even with snake boots."

"The first thing we can do is hack away the vines that are covering that hole where the top turret ripped out and take a look at the situation from up there."

In ten minutes, we had chopped a hole big enough to climb through. We struggled out of the fuselage and stood on the thick vines above it. Huldah had rolled north, leaving the sky overcast, but not with the thick storm clouds of yesterday. There were small scattered storms to the east, but the thin white layer now above us would follow Huldah, washing the sky bright blue by tomorrow. The wind had

136

faded. A flight of cattle egrets glided lazily eastward for a day's foraging among the farm fields.

My eyes moved downward, and my stomach did a double twitch. We were in the middle of an endless lake. The saw grass had disappeared completely, under at least six feet of water. The surface, broken only by other tree islands, stretched on and on to the distant woods we had struggled through three times yesterday, and the woods were flooded, too. Getting out of here looked impossible.

We had found Roy's ghost plane. We could prove that his claims were true. We could clear his name completely. But with miles of deep snake-infested water to cross and without any sort of boat, we were helpless.

13

WE STOOD ON TOP OF THE DENSE VINE MAT, staring at the water that stretched away from our island, too deep to wade through. And even if we did have the strength left to swim it, I knew what we would run into out there in the water and on any tree island where we might try to rest. The one we were on was already loaded with cottonmouths and rattlers.

"If you think we have a problem," Roy said, "I'm afraid I agree with you." He was flipping a little lump of crusty metal over and over in his hand. I'd almost forgotten the thing he'd stuck in his pocket when we'd first explored the old B-24.

"What is that, Roy?"

He held it out on his palm. I turned the thing over in my fingers. It was about two inches long and looked like two half-inch thick cylinders welded together side by side. One cylinder had a deep slot in it, and a piece of gas line was still wedged in there. The other section was plugged with what looked like a small light bulb base with the glass long since gone.

"I've got a mechanic's certificate," Roy said, "but I've never seen anything like that before. The fact that it was right at the fuel-line break got me to thinking. See the end of that little piece of tubing clamped in the slot?"

"Looks shiny."

"That's where I broke it off. I mean the other end. It's eaten away."

"That could be from sitting here thirty years."

"It could. The other side of it looks a bit like a small flashlight. I couldn't get that bulb base out without pliers, but I'll bet there's an old battery in there—"

"Hey, listen!"

On the light breeze, we heard the unmistakable cloppeting of a distant helicopter. I stood there wildly looking around for it. But Roy didn't waste a second.

"Got to find something that will burn. Quick."

Everything I could think of was too soggy to burn after last night's downpour.

"Don't you think he'll see us anyway?" I asked.

"We look big to us," Roy growled, "but to him, we're two gnats in a ten-mile-long jungle. Unless he flies right over us, he won't see a thing."

"How about burning our packs? That's all that's dry."

"Not big enough." He stomped around on the vines. "There's got to be something . . . something . . ."

139

"We could get out on the water if we had some kind of raft. Then the copter—"

I stopped because Roy had knocked the breath out of me with a tremendous slap on the back. "Hey, that's it! Chop away the vines over that hatch." He pointed at a little doorway a few feet behind the hole where the top gun turret had once been. Then he ducked back into the fuselage through the hole.

I began chopping. In a couple of minutes, I had cleared away the tendrils over the hatch. It jiggled and a corner popped loose. Roy was working the old releases from the inside. I stuck the machete blade under the corner and pried. The cover snapped off. Inside was a tightly folded bundle of faded yellow and gray plastic-looking stuff. Then I realized what it was. A life raft—and it was bone dry. That should burn just fine!

I pulled it out and broke open the crackly folds. The stuck-together mass opened into a pile of rubber-treated fabric about the size of a bushel basket. There was a metal bottle attached to it, like an aerosol can but with rounded ends and a toggle release. That was the carbon dioxide cylinder that would have inflated the raft when it was new, big enough to carry eight or ten men.

Roy scrambled out of the fuselage. "Yeah, that's good." He pulled off the CO_2 cylinder and threw it aside. "Let's drag it down the wing a ways, clear of the fuselage."

We heaped it on the vines just behind the left outboard engine, which I could make out beneath the leaves. Then we listened. The chopper was working the swamp maybe five miles west. Roy took the cap off his match container and touched flame to a cracked fabric edge. It licked along the ragged material of the old raft. The rubberized lining began to melt. The liquid rubber burned deep red and its smoke was black. A thin finger of it climbed off the hummock. Then the old raft really began to burn. A solid column of greasy smoke boiled high above us.

I couldn't hear the helicopter over the snap and rush of the fire, but Roy pointed west, and I saw it coming in low and fast.

Then the dark blue Air Force chopper hung a hundred feet above us, boiling the leaves in its hard downwash. A line snaked down, and at its end was a wide canvas loop. Roy lunged for it.

"Lift your arms," he ordered, and he tightened the canvas strap around my chest. "Hang on good," he yelled and waved up at the copter.

The winch up there began to reel in the line. The hummock dropped away beneath my boots, then turned slowly as I spun at the end of the line. Our smoke signal was flattened on the water by the rotor blast. I looked out over the Great Silver as I rose. It was a glittering lake. I could see that trying to swim out of there would have been hopeless.

Two pairs of hands pulled me out of the howling downwash into the big cave of the helicopter. I slipped out of the strap, and the line was let down again for Roy, the last one, after all, to leave his plane.

"Lucky thing you guys are out here," I shouted over the noise at one of the Air Force crewmen.

"Lucky, nothing!" a familiar voice back in the compartment yelled right back. I squinted into the shadows. There stood Al Derr.

"I had you fellas figured to a T," Al said when Roy was aboard, the big rescue door shut, and the helicopter scudding toward the base. "I knew you were heading for the Great Silver. When I called Aunt Agony, she told me you had high-tailed it out of there in Roy's car with a load of jungle gear. You didn't show up all night, so I put two and a few together, and I called the Air Force Base at Congaree. They picked me up at Blackwater, and here we are."

He looked at Roy and then at me. "You did find something, didn't you?"

"Found the bomber, Al," Roy said with a broad smile. "In fact, you were a hundred feet above it just now, and you didn't spot it. You see how well hidden it's been? Found my old crew in it. Just skeletons, now. It all happened like I said."

Al grabbed Roy's hand, shook it with his lips tight, and I saw tears glisten in the old man's eyes. The thud of the engine and slapping of the rotor blades closed in on us. Nobody said much of anything until the Air Force Air-Sea Rescue copter set us down on the ramp in front of the hangar at the base. Now there were handshakes all around. Then the radio operator motioned from his window. The crew piled back into the thing, and less than a minute later, the chopper whirred out of there to answer another rescue call.

The base was deserted. "We got a request from Civil Defense in Charleston for an observation plane. I sent Carl and Eddie over there with the Super Cub. There are floods all over the place. Dobbs Musserman is out somewhere with the loading truck to help people evacuate low areas. Harry and Frank are over near Columbia. They volunteered to help clean up some planes that were caught in a flash flood at an airport over there. I'm holding down the fort here by myself." He paused, then said as if he still didn't believe it, "Son of a gun, Roy. You actually found the bomber!"

I didn't want to think about it, but I figured one of those guys he had mentioned could have tried twice to knock Roy and me out of the search for the bomber the hard way—once with sabotage, and the second time by stealing our boat and leaving us marooned in a flood. Both times, he had nearly done it.

Al said, "You guys better get some sleep. Don't imagine you had much last night. Take my car. I'll catch a ride with one of the boys later. Roy, I expect you'll want to let the reporters in on what you found out there. If any of them happen to nose around out here, I'll just refer them to you."

We headed out of the base with Roy driving Al's old heap. "Funny thing," he said about the time we rolled past the old gatehouse, "but I'm not so eager to let the press in on this yet. The Air Force might put out a story, but I think they'll want to call me for a personal report before they do anything public. I'd say we have a few hours."

"For what?"

"To find out who tried to sidetrack us permanently. And why. Now let's work this out carefully so we waste as little time as possible. To start with, whoever it is doesn't know if we found anything or not. I figure he'll hang around to find out. Once he does, though, he'll head out of here like a scared rabbit and probably try to disappear for good."

"Why?"

Roy reached in his pocket and held up the odd little dual cylinder he'd brought from the bomber. "This."

"That?"

"I'm not sure, but I think it could be the key to the whole business, beginning way back in 1944. I'm hoping the FBI can tell me whether or not I've got an idea worth something. That's where I'm going right now. To the FBI in Charleston. And if I'm right, our sabotaging friend will be in a lot more trouble than he wants. That's why he's been trying so hard to keep us out of the Great Silver all along.

143

I'll drop you off at Aunt Agony's, and you can check with Art Ford by phone."

A half hour later, I was in Aunt Agony's parlor, and I had the Derby Airport manager on the phone. He wasn't too happy about it. "Where's my jeep?" he growled. "You guys never showed up last night, and Crimmins wants to know about his boat and trailer."

"The jeep's about two miles north of the Great Silver near a county road."

"That's just great," Art Ford said. "Full of rain, no doubt."

"We put the cover over it, but it's parked near a creek. It's probably full of swamp."

He began to sputter, and I said quickly, "Roy and I will put it back in shape for you. Roy's a mechanic. About the boat, though. It broke loose in the swamp. It's probably floating down the Wateree by now. Tell Mr. Crimmins we'll get it back for him—the trailer, too."

"Nice work," Ford said sarcastically. "Beautiful."

I decided to tackle the next subject head-on. "We've been so good to you," I said, "that maybe you'd like to do us a favor in return."

The phone was silent; then he began to chuckle. "Boy, you gotta lotta nerve!"

"Who did you call yesterday just as we drove out of there!"

"None of your business."

"Well, it could be, Mr. Ford. It just could be. I heard somebody in the swamp last night just before the storm broke. Now if he didn't make it out of there, you and I both might be talking with the state police before the day is out." What I said could be true enough, though I suspected the guy in the swamp had putted out of there, towing our boat, before the storm had caught up with him.

"Don't you threaten me, fella!" Art Ford said. But his voice had lost its cutting edge.

"I'm just telling you what could have happened."

There was another pause. Then he said, "Some guy called me and offered to send me twenty bucks for any tips I could give him on the phony bomber thing. That was just after you found the sawmill."

"What was his name?" I waited for the answer with my palm turning wet on the receiver. This could be it!

"Said it was Andrews," Ford said. "Never gave a first name."

"Andrews?" I repeated. A phony name, of course. But who was using it?

"Yep. I was to call him at a number he gave me. Say, you think I'll get the twenty spot?"

"What was the number?"

"Look, if you goof up the deal with Andrews—"

"I guess I'll have to ask the police—"

"O.K., O.K., the number is 337-8164 over in Charleston."

I thanked him, hung up, and paced around Aunt Agony's creaky old parlor. So I had a number and a brand-new name. Now what? I glanced at the flowered sofa, the shaky old chairs, and the old upright piano she never played. On top of the piano was one of those heavy cloths with fancy sewing on it and a few fading photographs in tarnished silver frames. I'd noticed them before, but not with any interest. One of them showed the house about thirty years ago. Another was of Aunt Agony herself in a skirt and sweater, standing in front of a hedge, smiling into the camera. She looked a lot younger than she did now. The third picture . . .

I picked it up and looked closely. The darndest feeling came over me.

Aunt Agony spoke from the doorway. "Storm blew every one of my bean vines loose. Had to tie 'em all back up. Did you make your call?"

Then she saw that I was interested in the photographs. "They don't mean much to you, I suppose. But I keep them around. An old woman's memories, you know. That one's the house just after we finished building it back in nineteen-ought-forty-two. And this one's me. My, that was a long time ago, wasn't it? And that one you're holding, that's one of the pictures Tod used to take out at the base. Used to photograph the crews in front of their planes, then take orders for prints from all the crew members."

Bingo! Things were falling into place. I took out my wallet and gave her a couple of dollars. "For the phone."

"But a call to Derby don't cost near that much."

"I'm going to call Charleston a couple of times, too."

I left word at the FBI office for Roy to call me at Aunt Agony's the minute he showed up; then I called the *Southeastern Advocate* and got hold of Knighton Reeves.

"Two things," I told him. "First, can you find out what kind of phone number 337-8164 is?"

"Has this any connection with that crazy bomber of Burnette's?"

I ignored that one. "Can you find out what that number is?"

"Why?"

"I just need a favor, that's all."

"I'll bet. What's the other one?"

146

"See who took the picture of Roy's bomber that day at Blackwater. Then call me here. I'll wait."

I gave him Aunt Agony's number. It took Reeves eight minutes.

"The number belongs to an answering service here in Charleston," Reeves said. Then he told me the name on the back of the photo of Roy and his crew that fatal day, the photo that was still in the newspaper's files as Ruthie Allen had told me. *Check!*

"What the heck is going on?" Reeves demanded.

"I'll let you know," I said. "Thanks a lot for this. I mean it." Before he could ask anything else, I hung up and gave Aunt Agony another fifty cents. "I'm setting up my own exchange," I said to her, and I called 337-8164.

"Give Mr. Andrews the message that there's something big going on in Blackwater," I told the answering service.

Aunt Agony said she'd wait for Roy's call, and I went back to my cabin, took a hot shower, and dug out clean slacks and a shirt. I'd set the trap and I felt good about it— for a few minutes. Then I realized that I might have set it for myself, and I didn't feel so good after all. I was glad to hear Aunt Agony tap on the cabin door and tell me that Roy was on the phone.

"Hey, I got something," he said before I could say much of anything. "One of the agents here described that gadget over the phone to Air Force Counter Intelligence at the Pentagon. They said that it sounded like a sabotage item used by enemy agents in World War II. They clamped in onto a gas line, and after a while some acid ate through the line. A few minutes after that, the acid cut a wire in the other part of the thing that closed the switch and, *wham,* a pen-cell battery set off a photo flashbulb like a shotgun

147

shell. We took the thing apart, and sure enough, there was a battery in there and the old bulb base was from a flashbulb."

"But flashbulbs don't explode and start gasoline fires."

"They sure do if you crack them first," Roy said. "The FBI is sending the gadget to Washington for analysis, but what they told me explains what happened to my B-24 and the crew. There'll be a full study of the wreckage, of course."

Then I told him what I'd found out about Tod Anthony. When I finished, he almost jumped through the phone.

"Do you realize what you might be getting into?" he shouted. "That guy plays rough! Listen to me, and listen good. I'm coming out there with the police. You stay put in that cabin until I get there, you hear me?"

"I can't do that, Roy. Not if that guy's as dangerous as you think."

"As I *think!* For Pete's sake, he tried to drop us into the swamp; then he marooned us there in a hurricane. How much of a threat do you need? Until he finds out that we've located the bomber and the whole thing's over for him, he'll still be trying to stop us."

"In that case, I'd be better off in a crowd, wouldn't I? I'm going to Moultrie's, and I'll stay right there until you get here."

He hung up with a groan, and I got into my car and drove the half a mile to Moultrie's.

Three cups of chickory later with only old man Moultrie himself as company, I began to think I had come up with a whole series of half-baked ideas that had fallen together into a nice set of coincidences.

"You want another cup?" Moultrie asked. The expression on his face made me wonder if anyone had ever survived four in a row.

I realized that some of the funny feeling in my stomach was the fact that I hadn't eaten anything since lunchtime yesterday. I ordered an egg sandwich. It came in from the kitchen the same time that Roy's car pulled up outside.

Only it wasn't Roy at all. It was Knighton Reeves with his gray face pulled down in the same old sour frown. He couldn't hide his excitement as well as he thought, though. His eyes were hard and shining.

"Had a hunch something big is going on out here, kid."

I didn't know whether I was glad or sorry to see him. I should have known he'd figure there was a story to be had after I'd called him about that phone number. "Have an egg sandwich?" I offered.

"Stop clowning."

"I'm not. I think we'd better mark time until Roy gets here from Charleston. He should be right behind you."

"You're not going to tell me anything?"

"Not without Roy."

Reeves shrugged his bony shoulders. "Then I'll have coffee and toast, Mr. Moultrie."

The toast came and went, then more coffee. We talked about the hurricane, mostly what it did in the Charleston area. I steered the conversation away from the Great Silver, and that wasn't easy. Reeves was a smart reporter, and he got some of his questions in almost before I realized what he was asking.

Then we heard a car pull in, and another right behind it. Into the restaurant walked The Beard, The Grizzly, and Scoop, the free-lance triplets.

I put my cup down because my hand had begun to shake

—just a little. And my mouth went dry. I picked up the cup again with both hands and took a bitter gulp.

"Uh huh," The Grizzly said. "There *is* something going on here. Reeves is never around for social reasons."

"How about it, Stewart?" Scoop said. "We gotta come up with something. Our editors want to cut this thing off. It's gone on too long."

I had four reporters facing me now. And one of them . . .

Then still another car crunched into the parking area. Roy at last! But again, it wasn't. Aunt Agony clumped into the place, nodded at all of us, and headed into the grocery store side of Moultrie's old building. "Buford," she called. "I need some vittles."

Buford Moultrie? I'd never heard his first name before. He wiped his hands on his apron and shuffled over to his grocery counter.

A muttered conversation had sprung up between Reeves and the free-lancers. "False alarm, eh?" The Grizzly said. "I was afraid of that. Not much use sticking around any more. I'm going back to the motel, check out, and go on to Daytona. I can pick up a few stories for the auto magazines. Nothing here. Nothing at all."

Scoop and The Beard stood up to leave with him. I knew that one of these three characters was wondering who had left a message for "Mr. Andrews" at the Charleston answering service, and why. But he couldn't do more than play along. This was no good. There were two things I could do to bring this affair to a head. One of them was to blurt out the news that Roy and I had found the bomber— the story that only Roy had the right to tell. They'd be all over me for the details, but then they'd rush for their typewriters. Three of them would. The other would disappear forever the minute he left Moultrie's, and I didn't think a guy who had murdered fourteen Air Force men should get away with it.

The other thing I could do was what I did. Aunt Agony walked toward the door with her bag of groceries. I got off the lunch-counter stool. "I want you to do me a favor," I told her. "These people are reporters, and they want to ask you about how it was here back in the 1940's."

She edged into the restaurant side of Moultrie's, looking nervous. But she wasn't half as nervous as I was.

"This is Mrs. Anthony," I began. "She owns some cabins at the west end of—"

"What is this?" Reeves said. "We don't need any more background."

"Nope, got it all," one of the free-lancers said.

But I was interested in the guy nearest the door. "How about you?" I asked him. "You got everything you need?"

He nodded. Aunt Agony's eyes swung toward him and stayed there.

"Didn't hear you," I said.

He nodded again. The others were looking at him oddly. Aunt Agony began to move nearer. Her mouth opened, but nothing came out. The whole thing hung in the balance now.

I said, "When I called 337-8164 a while ago—"

"Where'd you get *that* number?" the guy blurted out.

And his voice did it. *"It's him!"* Aunt Agony shrieked. *"It's him!"* Her grocery bag thudded to the floor. He whirled, slapped open the screen door, and was outside racing for his car before any of us could move. The engine howled, and the car spun out of Moultrie's parking lot, its tires kicking gravel against the old building like a charge of buckshot.

151

14

*W*E SPILLED OUT OF MOULTRIE'S, BUT OF
course we were too late to stop the car that by now was
bouncing eastward, screeching out of town fast.

Then its brake lights flashed. Beyond the escaping auto-
mobile, two cars had just jounced over the railroad tracks.
The lead car stopped. I saw that Roy had arrived at last.
The state police car behind him pulled around to block the
other lane.

The guy in the escape car tried to cut around the road-
block, but he forgot about the ditch that ran along both
sides of the road near the railroad tracks. The front wheels
leaped over the ditch, but the rear wheels sank in up to

their axles. Roy and the trooper jumped out of their cars and rushed toward the bogged-down auto. The rest of us dashed down the road to join them.

"As soon as I heard that voice," Aunt Agony gasped, "I knew it was Tod Anthony! After all these"—puff-puff—"years. Imagine!"

By the time we reached the car, the white-faced free-lance photographer had struggled from behind the wheel and was standing in the trooper's grip beside his car.

"Figured something was up as soon as I saw this guy roar away from Moultrie's and all you people pour out of there after him," Roy said. "So what you told me on the phone is true, Greg. The Beard here is really Tod Anthony!"

"All that spinach on his face was a good-enough disguise as long as he didn't say much and stayed away from Mrs. Anthony. I guess he dyed the beard and his hair to look a lot younger than he is."

The state trooper was confused. "I wish you all would explain what's going on here. It's a mite hard to make an arrest unless somebody's going to prefer charges."

"I will," Roy said. "With pleasure. I think suspicion of sabotage during wartime and two suspected attempts against my life and Stewart's ought to be enough to keep him around until the FBI and the Air Force make official charges."

The trooper stuck out his lower lip and nodded. "I'd say that ought to tangle him up pretty good. You come back to Charleston soon's you can to sign a statement."

"Gladly," Roy agreed, and the trooper led The Beard off to the patrol car.

We all went back to Moultrie's to pull ourselves together. The lack of sleep last night and the rugged hours in the swamp were beginning to catch up to me in a hurry. I tripped going up the steps, and Roy grabbed my arm.

"Easy, Greg. It's all over."

We collapsed in Moultrie's rickety chairs, and he put on a fresh pot of brew.

"That guy had been planting his little gadget on bombers that landed at Blackwater," Roy said. "Took pictures of their crews—that made him a familiar visitor. He needed only a minute when no one was looking to duck into the bomb bay and snap the gadget in place."

"Gadget? What gadget?" The Grizzly said. The reporters were beginning to realize there was a big story here after all.

"You can't release a thing until it's cleared by the FBI," Roy warned, "but you fellows can come back to Charleston with me and I'll do what I can for you."

"Something tells me," Knighton Reeves began, "something tells me that you found that bomber."

"Off the record, until it's officially cleared, something tells me you're right," Roy admitted.

"When? Where? How?" the three reporters exploded at once.

"Wait a minute!" Roy grinned. "I'll give you all the details in Charleston the minute it can be released. There's a lot more to it besides finding the plane."

"What I don't get," I said, "is why Anthony came back here. Sure, the flashbulb base in the gadget pointed right at him, but who knew where he was? Why didn't he just stay away and keep his mouth shut?"

Roy grinned at Aunt Agony. "Tell him why, Mrs. Anthony."

She frowned at him. Then her eyebrows climbed right into her gray hair. "Oh, my stars! The support checks he has

154

to send me! Why I've had him tracked down every time he forgot to mail one."

"It's not so easy to disappear," Roy said. "Not with Social Security, credit bureaus, and all. Besides, he had no reason to disappear if the bomber was never found. Came down here first to see if there was anything to the rumors he must have read in the national wire service stories. Then he got worried that I might be onto something, and he tried to stop me and Greg."

Reeves opened his mouth to say something, but suddenly the whole building shook in a tremendous wind blast. Huge drops of rain popped on the roof.

"Rotten weather!" Scoop muttered. "Changes every ten minutes."

"Don't knock it," Roy said. "If it wasn't for a sudden weather change thirty years ago, I would have flown out over the Atlantic on the original flight plan and never been heard from again. That's how Anthony was getting away with it. Probably collected a fee from the enemy for each plane he knocked down. But my flight was turned back over land by a weather change right after takeoff. That's why the bomber is in the Great Silver instead of at the bottom of the ocean with the other two. That's why Greg and I were able to find out what had really happened to it."

Aunt Agony's voice came out of the silence that followed Roy's words. "I told Tod he'd get into trouble with that camera of his. . . . So that's why he left so quick. Day after that third bomber went down, come to think of it."

"He was afraid it would be found and the sabotage traced to him," Roy said. "He took up a new life and then figured he was in the clear. But a few weeks ago, he must have read or heard about my search for the bomber. He had to come back to see if there really was a chance of finding it. Then when we began to use the MAD, he got good and scared. That's when he tried to stop us."

The Grizzly, Scoop, and Reeves began shouting questions all at once. Roy held up both hands. "In Charleston with the FBI, you guys. In Charleston. Mr. Moultrie, my friend, let's have coffee all around. I'm buying."

I began to wonder if anybody would believe any of this back in Pennsylvania. I took a sip of Moultrie's one and only original blend. Amazing. That last cup of Buford Moultrie's bone-rattling coffee didn't taste bad at all!

VOYAGER BOOKS